Darkest Fears
Boo

*A Christmas Wish*

CLAIR DELANEY

# DARKEST FEARS TRILOGY REVIEWS

*'Read all three books in two days. Such a roller coaster of emotions and so drawn into the story. Love Coral and Tristan and that they're a mature couple.' Amazon*

*'Love, love, love these books!' iBooks*

*'Magnificent! From the beginning this was so hard to put down. Epic romance. This author has become one of my favourites!' Kobo*

*'Awesome story.' Barnes & Noble*

*'This is a fantastic series that delivers on its ability to both excite and entertain. You won't be disappointed.' Amazon*

*'I loved these books. I couldn't put it down, I finished the trilogy in a few days.' iBooks*

*'Great, really enjoyed the books.' Barnes & Noble*

*'Darkest Fears Trilogy is a set of books with a story that will hold the attention of the reader from the beginning to the end of the third book.' Amazon*

*'Wow…what an utterly compelling story. Clair Delaney is now one of my top 10 authors. I looking forward to reading more of her books in the future.' iBooks*

*'I thought the trilogy was well written, exciting and all came together in the end. Good page turner for me! I'd highly recommend it!' Amazon*

# ALSO BY CLAIR DELANEY

**Fallen For Him**
Darkest Fears Trilogy Book One

**Freed By Him**
Darkest Fears Trilogy Book Two

**Forever With Him**
Darkest Fears Trilogy Book Three

# CONTENTS

One ............................................................................ 1
Two ........................................................................... 14
Three ........................................................................ 27
Four .......................................................................... 37
Five ........................................................................... 50
Six ............................................................................. 59
Seven ........................................................................ 68
Eight ......................................................................... 78
Nine .......................................................................... 93
Ten .......................................................................... 105
Eleven ..................................................................... 115
Twelve ..................................................................... 121
Thirteen .................................................................. 132
Christmas Eve ........................................................ 144
Epilogue .................................................................. 156
About the Author ................................................... 164

# ONE

December 2013

I AM SAT CROSS-LEGGED on the sofa in the library, staring down at the fire burning brightly. I was supposed to be taking it easy today, and reading Dan Brown's Inferno, the new book I bought, but I can't concentrate. It's Saturday morning, and Tristan is already hard at work in his office, he said it's because he has so much to do in preparation for us going away in January to Hawaii – it's still not sunk in yet that we are actually going. I am so excited, yet very nervous too.

I dreamily gaze out of the window, it's pouring down, rain lashing hard against the windows, and my mind wonders back in time again to the day I first met Tristan, and how quickly I fell in love with him. We've been together for five blissful months now, admittedly seems like a lot longer, but in a good way – as life with Tristan just keeps getting better and better. I'm healing more each day, on the inside and outside, and I know it's only been possible with Tristan's help, his love, and his patience.

Then I think of everything else that's happened this year – My Mom passing away, and all the craziness with Susannah, which led to her...leaving us, and then Danny saving us both from Kane. Rob & Carlos having that scare and then becoming parents. Gladys and Malcolm getting hitched, Joyce losing John then selling up and now living in Florida. Scott & Debs almost splitting, which they haven't thank god, Tristan's ex-girlfriend Olivia trying to get him back, my ex-boyfriend Justin trying to get me back. Leaving Brighton, flying for the first time, having my very first holiday in Cornwall with Tristan, my new career courtesy of Tristan, and leaving my studio.

Which makes me think of Bob, and in turn, I feel an ache inside, as every now again, I have missed my life at the studio, and seeing Bob every day, I miss our daily chats. I start to feel a little melancholy, so I decide I will pop over and see him today, even though he was here on Thursday night for tea - I can't help worrying about him.

I feel another wave of melancholy about Bob wash over me and I know I'm being silly. He's fine down there, as he has told me, on several occasions, so I take a deep breath, and clear my mind of all those things that can get me feeling off-kilter, and think about the present moment.

Christmas is literally around the corner, well not literally – ok so it's the 5$^{th}$ of December tomorrow, which doesn't leave many days for all the things that I should be doing. And it's my first Christmas with Tristan, as a married woman – I still have to pinch myself that it's true. That I have Tristan, that I live here, and that we are bonded to one another now, no matter what.

My belly flutters again at the thought of my lovely husband, and for the fact that for the first time in my life, I have a Christmas wish, something that I want. I stopped wishing a long time ago, even though Gladys tried her best to make Christmases magical when I was a kid - and even as an adult – I guess I was just too much of a mess to really appreciate what she was trying to do.

So, I have decided that I'm going to host Christmas this year, which I've never done before. But as I explained to Tristan last night when I told him of my wish – which he is not too happy about - I want to show my family and friends how much I love and care for them, and how grateful I am for all their help this year. In caring for us both during our recovery; supporting us in our very deep romance that quickly turned to marriage, and for just being there.

But most importantly, I want Tristan to have a full-on family Christmas, I want to show him that even though his folks are gone, he has a family again and that he's not alone. I know it affects him more than he says or shows, but now I'm coming to the realisation of how much I actually have to do, and to be honest, I'm having a bit of a meltdown about it. Which is kind of annoying, because it's exactly what Tristan said would happen. He thinks it's too much with all that's happened this year, citing '*I am still healing*', which is true, but I really want to do this. So I decide to sit calmly, with pen and paper and write everything down, that way I can't fuck it up by forgetting anything.

Firstly, Tristan and I have no Christmas Decorations, no twinkly lights, tinsel or Christmas Trees. Which is terrible, as

Gladys always had them up on the 1st December, but Tristan and I have been so busy, I just haven't stopped to think about it. So that's first thing tomorrow – shopping for the above.

Tristan is then away for two days, so I'm hoping as it's such a big house, that Edith will help me decorate before she heads to Devon for the holidays. Otherwise, I may still be at it come Christmas Eve!

Secondly, actual presents – *Haven't bought a damn thing!* So I definitely need to get Edith's present sorted tomorrow too, as she's away the day after, the same as Tristan. I don't even want to begin thinking about how strange the house is going to feel without them both here - quiet and empty, that's how - I frown at the pen and paper in my hands, and re-read the list.

*Christmas Decorations*
*Christmas Presents*

I then decide that the next most important thing on the list is food. Party food for Christmas Eve and then a Turkey with all the trimmings for Christmas Day, then I think, if I don't know who is coming, then how am I to know how much food to buy?

*God this hosting thing is stressful!*

Ignoring that thought, I add 'food' to the list. Then deciding I need some expert help from Gladys, *and* her recipes as she always makes everything from scratch including Christmas pudding and mince pies, I get to my feet. As I enter the main living area I hear Christmas Carols playing very loudly – Ding Dong Merrily On High to be precise. Edith must have the radio on.

As I pass the kitchen I see Edith, she hasn't noticed me and is singing at the top of her voice to the Christmas Carol, which makes me giggle to myself – Then I wonder if Tristan is actually managing to get any work done? Still laughing at the scenario, I grab my fury, knee-length winter boots that Tristan bought for me from the utility room, and head back over to the kitchen.

"Edith!" I shout, trying to gain her attention over the warbling going on. "Edith!" I shout again, as I'm pulling my boots over the top of my jeans.

She finally spins around with a big smile on her face and turns the radio down. "Oh hello lass, I didn't see you there," she says, her cheeks pink from her extravagant singing, and if I didn't know better I'd say Edith's been on the wine too, but hey, who I am I to judge – *It's Christmas!*

"I'm off out for a while, do you need me to pick anything up on my way back?" I ask.

"No lass, I did the grocery shopping yesterday," she says. I really do love her Scottish accent.

I smile fondly at her. "Ok, see you later. I'm on my mobile if you need me."

"Alright lass, have fun," Edith smiles warmly, then returns to whatever it is she's cooking up, which makes me stop and turn back around.

I sigh, feeling guilty. "Edith, you're not supposed to be cooking at weekends," I softly scold.

"Oh, I know. I'm just stocking up the freezer for when I'm away. That way, you and Tristan won't have so much to do," she replies jubilantly. My heart melts - she really is one of the kindest people I have ever known.

I walk into the kitchen and give her a big bear hug. "You're a superstar Edith, you know that?" I say smiling warmly at her.

"Ah, away with you," she says, her cheeks flushing red – I think I've embarrassed her.

I smile again, then I remember my plan. "Can I ask for a favour Edith?" I say, hoping she'll say yes.

"Whatever you need," she replies, as she stirs the big pot in front of her – I think it's a casserole?

"Well, I wanted to ask, would you mind helping me decorate the house before you go away? It's just it's so big and' – "I'd love to," she interrupts, 'we can have a sing-song as we go from room to room," she suggests, her tone excited.

I grin widely at her. "Sounds like fun, and thanks, Edith." *Phew!*

"Not a problem," she says with a smile.

As I walk back down the hallway, towards Tristan's office, Edith turns the radio back up and continues singing her Christmas Carols, which brings a big smile to my face. I knock on Tristan's office door, not really sure if he'll be able to hear me over the music, or Edith's singing!

"Come," I hear him shout – which instantly reminds me of Joyce.

My mood sinks a little as I think of her, and all that happened. I really wish she was going to be here for Christmas, but I also understand her reasons for not wanting to do that – too many memories of John, which makes my heart constrict for her – I hope she's doing better. And with that thought, I decide to try calling her again tomorrow as we keep missing each other. Feeling down about Joyce and John, and knowing Joyce wouldn't want me to be, I close my eyes for a second, pick myself back up and enter Tristan's office.

He's sat in his large leather chair, and he's on a call. His face is serious as he nods and listens intensely. He's dressed casually in dark blue jeans and a black, long-sleeved t-shirt that hugs him in all the right places, and his medium brown hair is all dishevelled, making him look deliciously scrumptious and very sexy.

He glances up and seeing me, his face instantly changes. His big chocolate brown eyes widen and turn a softer shade of brown. His frown disappears, and a smile begins to spread across his face. He motions me forward with his left hand, his wedding ring shining brightly as he does, and he keeps it there, held out to me. I smile in return, close the door behind me and skip towards my lovely, sexy, sweet husband.

Reaching him I place my right hand in his, and he pulls me forward, so I fall sideways onto his lap, which makes me chuckle. I wrap my right arm around his neck and taking in his gorgeous scent, I kiss his exposed neck. It sends shivers to all the right places – and I'm instantly taken back to this morning, and our frolicking around in bed. Which in all honesty, I thought would fade, as it did with Justin, but if anything, our chemistry for one another has only intensified. It's far stronger and much deeper than I would have thought possible, and I ponder that thought - Maybe it's because we are both settled now, and have what we both needed and wanted?

His voice pulls me from my musing. "It does sound like a good investment. What's your estimate on the return?" He asks and listens intently to the reply. Yet his hand is squeezing my waist, making me feel wanted and welcome, even though he's hard at work. I place my left hand on his and play with his wedding ring. I really do find it very sexy that it represents me, and our deep love for one another.

"Hmm...I see, let me take another look at the figures. I think it could' – He listens again, and nods several times. "I understand that Yanif, but I won't take that much of a risk, not anymore." He looks up at me, and all I can see is love and desire. It stirs my very soul.

"Alright...and I agree. Let me come back to you in say...' he looks down at his watch, 'an hour." He says then listens for a few more seconds before finally ending the call.

"Hi," I whisper and kiss his neck again.

"Hi," he smiles widely at me, his eyes crinkling sweetly at the corners. Then he cups the back of my neck with his hand, pulls me towards him and kisses me, his tongue lapping gently against mine.

I moan as I sink into the kiss. His scent, his touch, his pure love and adoration for me, are making my legs shake, even though I'm sat on his lap. He pulls back, and we stare at one another for a moment, soft chocolate brown eyes to coral blue, and I know he can feel it too, the love bubble that still surrounds us.

"I am a very lucky girl," I whisper, as I caress his cheek.

He takes my hand and kisses the inside of my palm. "No, I'm the lucky one," he tells me.

I smile widely at his words. "You're busy," I say as I scan his desk, there's lots of paperwork laid out in front of him. "Although, how you're actually managing to get any work done with' – "Edith's singing?" Tristan interrupts, smiling widely.

"Yes," I chuckle.

"It's no bother," he says, his warm chocolate eyes smiling back at me.

"So what are you working on?" I ask, as ever I am always interested in what he does, not that I understand it all.

"There are plans for a new development on the Marina, luxury apartments. They won't be built until 2017, but it does sound like a good investment." He says, and I can tell he's deep in thought about it.

"How much will they cost, the apartments?" I ask – wondering if it's something we should look at buying ourselves. I miss being so close to the water, the smell, the sound of the waves, and even though I love this house, I'm starting to think it won't really be practical for when we start a family – I'll be up and down the stairs all day and night!

*Maybe a big bungalow would suit us?*

He smiles, but his one eyebrow is cocked up in curiosity. "Why do you ask?"

I feign innocence, I haven't shared those thoughts with him yet because, in all honesty, I'm not sure *when* the whole having a baby thing is going to happen, I'm too busy enjoying having him to myself.

"Just curious,' I shrug, 'and you know...making sure you get your monies worth," I add, as though I know what the hell I'm

## A Christmas Wish

talking about, which I don't. Money, investments, and profit margins are not my forte.

He smiles widely at me and chuckles once. "There's going to be eleven new towers, which will create 853 new homes. A one bedroom apartment will be around the five hundred thousand mark' – "Five hundred thousand!" I interrupt, my voice high pitched, 'that's ridiculous!" I squeak, thoroughly shocked, my mouth gaping open in horror. *Jeez!*

Tristan grins widely at me again. "They *are* luxury apartments my darling, which will be built to the highest specifications and to the kind of clientele they will attract, that's like spare change to them."

I quickly close my mouth, knowing he's right. I just feel like the poor are getting poorer, and the rich, richer. Which makes me feel a little guilty, but then again, I have to remember how much Tristan contributes to charities, and building homes for the poor, so at least I can say that he, no scratch that, we may be rich, but at least we do our bit to help.

"And are they all one bedroom?" I ask.

He squeezes me around the waist and smiles again. "No, one, two and three bedrooms, and of course the penthouse," he tells me.

I roll my eyes. "You mean the pimp house," I reply dryly, which makes Tristan burst into laughter.

It takes him a while, but he finally speaks again. "Why would you say that?" he asks, still chuckling.

I shrug. "It sounds like a pimp house, 'the penthouse', you know...I just imagine some guy, who thinks he's all that, the kind of male tart that would want one of those just so he can impress the girls that he brings back to his *'penthouse'* and they fall for it..." I stop talking because he's looking at me that way again. "What?" I laugh.

"I really do love the way your mind works," he says, 'don't ever change baby," he adds, smiling adoringly at me.

I can't help chuckling. "I won't, I promise."

"Good." And we're kissing again – It never seems to be enough. As the kiss slows down, I pull back and gaze at him. "So come on, tell me what ridiculous price would one have to pay for *'the penthouse'*?" I ask with a chuckle.

He's serious again. "It's not too bad actually, just under 1,2," he says – he's talking money language again.

I cock an eyebrow up at him. "And that means...?"

"One million, two hundred thousand," he tells me.

"And that has four bedrooms?" I ask.

"No three," he replies.

"And how much are the three beds?" I ask.

"Depends on what model you choose, but they're going to start at around five-nine and go up to eight," he tells me.

I think I have the hang of this money talk. "So, it's five hundred and ninety thousand, with the top one being eight hundred thousand?" I question.

"Correct my darling," he tells me, his voice singing with pride.

I frown as I think about that. "But why pay for a penthouse that only has three beds, when you can get a three bed for hundreds of thousands less?" I ask, wondering if it's a silly question.

"It's a good question," Tristan praises, 'but you have to remember baby, you're getting the whole of the top floor with the penthouse, it's a hell of a lot more square footage compared to the three bed," he says.

I nod my head, I hadn't thought of that. "True," I say, 'so do you think you're going to invest?" I ask.

"We," he corrects me.

I roll my eyes. "Yes darling – we," I reply sarcastically.

He wraps his other arm around me and turns slightly, so we're almost nose to nose. His eyes are penetrating through me that way again, strong, bold, dark and intense. "When are you going to get used to the fact that all this is yours too?" He asks; his tone serious.

I sigh inwardly. "I don't know Tristan..." I shake my head, 'probably never," I add, laughing at myself.

His eyes close, and he leans his forehead against mine. "All that is mine is yours," he whispers, reciting what he told me in Cornwall.

I close my eyes too, savouring the moment. "I know," I whisper back, 'it just takes some getting used to,' I add. "Please don't be mad at me," I beg, remembering our one and only fight about money that happened in Cornwall before we were married...

I AM STANDING before him with my arms crossed, and my foot tapping, feeling way beyond mad. How can he not see my point of view, or more to the point, at least hear me out? "Tristan!" I say his name again, feeling totally exasperated with him. How much longer are we going to be fighting about this – it's ridiculous!

"Absolutely not! No Coral. I will not agree to this. End of." He tells me again.

He's fuming, well so am I.

I narrow my eyes at him. "Tristan, will you at least hear my side of the argument?"

"This isn't an argument or a debate. I will not budge on this Coral. And I won't say it again, this conversation is over." His voice is sharp and to the point. I feel like a child that's being scolded.

"You are not the boss of me!" I can't help raising my voice. And some sadistic side of me wants to laugh out loud at myself because he *is* my boss.

"No, I'm not. But I damn well have the right to do whatever I want with my wealth. You have no say in this!" He shouts.

"But I want a say in this!" I shout back.

Yet again, we are two angry fools, glaring at one another.

I take a deep breath to attempt to get this out in the right way. "Tristan, think of the consequences, the what ifs? That's all it needs. Couples get divorced all the time. Just because we love each other, it doesn't make us immune you know!" I shout, my teeth clenching together.

He takes a deep calming breath with closed eyes – he really is mad.

Then, taking a step towards me, he takes hold of both of my hands in his and bends slightly, so we are eye to eye. "Ok, for the last time. I do understand your point of view, I really do. But if we were – god forbid – to divorce, then I would want you taken care of' – "I can take' – 'care of yourself. Yes. You have expressed this on several occasions, to the point of annoyance. I am well aware of how strong and independent you are it's one of the many things about you that I fell in love with. But I mean it Coral, there's no more discussion to be had." He stares back at me, his face dead serious. I want to stamp my feet like a child. Instead, I pull my hands out of his and start pacing the room.

"That's not fair," I bite back, defiantly.

"Fair or not fair. You are not having a prenuptial agreement, I won't allow it." He says, his voice firm – I imagine it's what he used to sound like in court, as a barrister. Strong, firm and very intimidating, but I won't let it sway me, I have to stand firm.

"And what if I get my own prenuptial agreement made?" I say, my head held high, thinking how clever I am for coming up with that thought.

"It wouldn't stand up in court darling. I'm the wealthy one, not you." *Ugh, he is so annoying sometimes!*

"Tristan, don't you see? I'm trying to protect you." I say, my tone begging.

"I don't need protecting. And I don't see why you can't get your head around the fact that when we marry, actually even now, all that is mine is yours, and always will be." He argues back.

"That's not fair. If we divorced, I wouldn't want any of your money." I state firmly, hating the thought of not being with him. "Why should I get any of your hard earned money? It's not mine to have. You made that money before I ever met you. It's yours, not mine!" I shout, totally exasperated with him.

Tristan sighs heavily and mumbles to himself. I think he said *'for the love of god'*, but I'm not sure. He sits on the edge of the sofa, places his elbows on his knees, folds his hands together and rests them against his mouth. He's staring out of the window – and I know he's contemplating something, but what I don't know – So I take this as my opportunity to be really honest, even though it's scary.

Kneeling down in front of him, I look up at him. "I'm afraid," I tell him solemnly.

His eyebrows knit together in concern. "What are you afraid of baby?" He asks, his demeanour softening. I shake my head, it's so hard saying what I feel, but I know I must, so I take a deep breath and begin.

"I'm afraid...that everyone is going to think that I only married you because you're rich. I'm afraid that unless *I* do this, *you'll* think I only married you because you're rich. And I'm afraid that people will think that I seduced...or tricked you into a quick marriage so I could get my hands on your money." I take another breath, find some courage from somewhere, and continue.

"A prenuptial agreement will put my mind at rest, and hopefully, any fears or doubts you may secretly have about my true feelings. And people will know that I never married you for money, I married you because I fell in love with you." There, I said it. I look up at him, only to find he looks shocked.

He reaches down and places his hands either side of my face. His intense look is back, it really does shake my foundations when he looks at me like that, like he would die for me.

"Not for a second, have I ever doubted your true feelings for me. Believe me, baby, I have met so many women who just want to be a trophy wife, and will only marry for money. They want the luxury, the lifestyle, the clothes, the holidays, the jewellery – You are not them, in any way, it's just not possible. You are the most genuine, real, honest woman I have ever met in my life. I have fallen in love with you Coral Stevens, and I want you to be my wife, and if that means that you automatically become rich too, then so be it. I don't give a damn what anyone thinks." He gently strokes my cheek then continues.

"Besides, look at it this way, who do you know that would think like that? People you don't even care about, that's who. The people that do matter, your family and friends, know that you would never marry for money. And that my darling, is all you should be concerned about. So can we please agree that we will not be partaking in a prenuptial agreement? Please, baby, I'm begging you," he says, his voice totally sincere.

I sigh heavily. I don't want to give in to this, and I know Tristan can see my reluctance, so he continues.

"Coral, if we had one, and something happened to me, which would mean you were left with nothing, how could I say I ever cared for you? Don't you understand? It's my duty to provide for you, and it will be my honour to be your husband, and the father of our children, so please don't take this away from me. I need to know that if something happened to me, you and our future children would be taken care of. It would give me peace of mind, and I'll feel far more content knowing you'll be ok if the worst happened, not struggling because of some stupid piece of paper." He takes a breath and gazes down at me with softer, chocolate brown eyes.

"Please Coral, stop fighting me and let's agree that we don't need a prenuptial agreement. Please...please darling," he begs.

Tears spring to my eyes. I can't even begin to think about him not being in my life. I am lost for words, so I just nod my head once. Tristan leans his forehead against mine for a moment, then his lips reach mine, and the argument is forgotten...

"MAD?" HE ASKS, sitting up straight as his eyes search mine.

I sigh outwardly. "Yeah mad...I'm trying Tristan, I really am. It's taken time, but I've only just got used to having Edith around, everything else...' I shake my head again, thinking about my new car, the yacht, my own business, this wonderful big house. "I just need time baby, for it all to sink in," I say, and place my hands against his cheeks. "Hey...you got me to agree on not having a prenuptial agreement didn't you, isn't that enough?" I ask.

He looks a little guilty. "I had a fair point," he says.

I cock an eyebrow up. "You're a damn good barrister, that's what you are. No wonder you always won, you're very convincing when you want to be," I say, smiling at him.

His face falls, and he's suddenly intense. "Every word I said was true," he states passionately.

And now I feel guilty for saying that he convinced me using his mad skills.

I look down and shake my head. "I'm sorry Tristan, I didn't mean it the' – "I know you didn't," he softly says, and we stare at one another again, the small difference of opinion forgotten. He smiles widely at me, my face automatically responds with a wide smile of my own, and my guilt is forgotten.

"Did you need something baby? Or were you missing me?" He asks, giving me a little squeeze. And I also know this is his way of subtly telling me he needs to get on, he's a very busy man.

I lean forward and peck his lips again. "I always miss you when I'm not with you," I tell him, 'but I did have something I wanted to ask you," I say, feeling lighter and happy.

"What's that?" he says, his tone playful.

"Would you like to come shopping with me tomorrow? Or are you too busy?" I ask.

"Shopping? I thought Danny took Edith yesterday?" he says, serious again.

"He did, I meant Christmas shopping, just for decorations and Edith's present. We could go first thing, it shouldn't be too busy, and then Edith said she's going to help me decorate the house, so at least you can get back to work," I say.

"Are you trying to get rid of me?" he teases.

I smile coyly at him. "Yes," I tease back.

"And what, may I ask, makes you think I don't want to do any decorating?" he asks.

"You do?" I squeak, surprised.

He's intense again. "Coral, darling, this is our first Christmas together, our first Christmas in this house, our first Christmas as husband and wife. I want to decorate the house with you. Especially the tree...I always loved trimming the tree..." He drifts for a moment, and I know he's thinking about his folks. Suddenly he looks up at me and gently places his hands on my cheeks. "There are so many reasons to celebrate this year..." he says.

"Yes,' I whisper, moved by the moment, "There are many reasons, my love," I lean down and plant my lips on his.

Edith knocks the door, interrupting us. "Come in," Tristan shouts.

# TWO

EDITH WALKS INTO the office and smiles widely at Tristan – Sometimes I think she's happier than me that we met. Or maybe it's her motherly love for Tristan that makes her so pleased to see him happy?

"Is everything alright Edith?" Tristan asks, his hand secretly squeezing my butt cheek - I try to keep a straight face.

"Yes,' she says, 'you wanted some brunch when I finished with the Casserole," she reminds him.

*The man still eats like a horse – And I was right, Casserole, yummy!*

"So what would you like?" she adds.

"Coral?" Tristan asks. *Is he kidding?*

Tristan seems to be under the impression that since our scare with Kane, I have lost my appetite. I have tried to explain to him many, many times, that my lack of appetite has nothing to do with Kane, and everything to do with being in love with him, but he just looks at me shakes his head at me. In fact, I would go so far as to say he doesn't believe me, which is really annoying. *Ugh! He is one stubborn man!*

"I'm not eating!" I tell him firmly.

He instantly looks frustrated with me. "Coral' – "Edith,' I say and look up at her, 'can you give us a second?" I ask nicely – and I know she can tell that Tristan's about to get it.

"Of course," she says, and she can't scuttle out of his office quickly enough.

I'm up onto my feet in a flash, my hands on my hips as I stare down at him still sat in the chair. His face looks contrite like he knows he's about to be told off – and so he should be!

"Stop it, Tristan. It's 10.30 in the morning. I ate one hour ago. I am not hungry, so, therefore, I will not be eating again." I try to keep my cool, but he really is driving me crazy with the eating thing. I know I'm going to have to sit down at some point, when he's not working, and talk rationally to him about it.

He sighs heavily as his hand comes up to his mouth, his forefinger tapping his top lip. He's contemplating something, I know that. But as we continue to stare intensely at one another, I start to wither under his gaze. All of a sudden I'm feeling hot and flustered, yet shy and self-conscious too like I did when we first met.

*How can he still affect me like this?* - He notices this, and his head cocks to the side as a very sexy smile starts to spread across his face. *Ugh! He's winning, wearing me down with his sexiness!*

"Don't look at me like that!" I tell him. I am not in the mood for games, but I feel the smile beginning to form on my face – *God damn it!*

His grin widens. "Like what?" he teases in his most sexy voice.

"Tristan!" I warn.

He stands fluidly, quickly, making me catch my breath. His look is so heated, his eyes dark. "Yes?" he questions, upping the stakes.

I automatically take a step back as a wonderful frisson of excitement floods my body, making my heart race, and my breathing speed up. "What do you want?" I ask, my voice trembling slightly, giving me away.

"You," he says, taking another step towards me, a prowler about to catch his prey.

"Well, you can't!" I tease, and take another step back – *This is fun and sexy!*

"Why not?" He questions and steps forward again. My heart is pumping loudly against my chest, I want to scream in a girly way and run, knowing he'll catch me.

I take a deep rasping breath. "Because you drive me crazy – that's why!" I pant, a little of the frustration I felt a moment ago coming back.

He smiles coyly at me and closes the distance between us a little more, we are only a few feet away from each other now. "And you'll deny me this moment, this kiss?" he says, sending his scent towards me. I look down and see he's well past turned on; his erection is very visible as it tries to break free from his jeans.

"That's all you want – a kiss?" I question seductively. Feeling well and truly turned on too.

"Yes, a kiss," he whispers.

And I'm about to launch myself at him, and have mad, crazy sex on his desk, but right at that moment, I get a flashback. I haven't had one in weeks – and Tristan's on the floor in the pool room, and I can't get him breathing, he won't wake up – It's the only nightmare that plagues me now, although I try my best to hide it from him.

"Coral?" He questions, concerned now.

I shake my head and try to push the image away, but it won't go – *No!*

"Baby," he's instantly over to me and wraps me up in his arms. I reciprocate, my arms clutching tightly to his back. I squeeze my eyes shut and rest my head on his chest, as I try to calm myself down, and bring my breathing back to normal. "I've got you," he adds, as he gently rocks me.

"I'm sorry," I croak.

"You didn't do anything wrong Coral," he softly tells me.

"I spoiled the game," I whisper, squeezing him tighter, the image is finally fading. *Thank god!*

"No you didn't," he tells me firmly and plants a sweet kiss on the top of my head. "Coral, you haven't had a moment like this in weeks, so don't be so hard on yourself. You've changed so much since I met you, and I wish you would give yourself more credit for that." I feel his lips kiss my hair again and inhale deeply. "I think you are incredible, and you have fantastic smelling hair," he adds lightly, which makes me chuckle - And I love him so much for making me feel better.

"Thanks," I squeak, smiling a little now.

"Want to talk about it?" He softly asks, rubbing his hands across my shoulders and back. I know he does this because he's worked out that it comforts me.

"No thanks," I whisper, feeling guilty for not sharing.

"Alright," he says and kisses the top of my head again.

And now he waits, patiently, for whatever it is I need. You see, Tristan and I have developed a pattern, as most couples do I guess. If I'm in his arms and I'm upset, he doesn't move an inch. It's like he knows I need to be held for a long time, and he does this for me, without complaint, although I think he might like it too. And whenever he asks if I want to talk about it, and I don't, he doesn't ask again, he lets it go. It's like he knows when to push and when not to, and I would go so far as to say he knows the difference between a memory invading my thoughts, and some silly fear about the future – *God I love him for this!*

"Thank you, baby," I whisper, giving him another squeeze. Then, resting my chin on his chest, I look up into his warm, soulful eyes.

"Better?" he softly asks, as he takes my face in his hands, and lightly kisses my lips.

"I am now," I softly say. I seem to recover far quicker than I ever have from moments like these. I know it's all down to Tristan and his love for me.

He smiles softly as he silently runs his fingers through my hair, and then he becomes serious again, in fact, I'd say a little sad.

"What are you looking so sad about?" I whisper, searching his face for the answer. His eyebrows scrunch together, and he shakes his head once, so I know I'm right, he was sad for a moment.

"Sometimes," he whispers, 'I am blown away by the fact that you are mine, my love. I never thought I would have this," he adds, and I'm sure he's referring to his old beliefs, and his shaken confidence.

And I know there's so much more to him losing his folks and being alone that he's never told me about, and that's ok, I'll never push him to share what he doesn't want to, but like him with me, I just wish I could take it away for him. I close my eyes to his sweet words, rest my head on his chest for a second then look up at him, wanting to cheer him up, the way he's cheered me up.

"Ok, so you want to tell me what you're hungry for?" I ask with a smile, feeling back to where I was before that...*moment.*

His one eyebrow cocks up. "How about you tell me why you have your boots on?" he asks, his mood also lighter.

"Oh...I'm off to see mom and dad so I can invite them over for Christmas," I say. "And then I'm going to see Bob," I add, remembering at that moment to call before I head over, as I swear Gladys and Malcolm have been at it the couple of times I've popped over unannounced, and I do not want to catch them at it again – ever.

Tristan looks annoyed. "You're supposed to be taking it easy today," he lightly scolds.

I think he keeps forgetting that I recently promoted Lucy to Supervisor at the sandwich shop Tristan bought for me, which is more like a swanky snack bar now, and hired another full-time member of staff because since all the changes I suggested were implemented, business is booming.

"Yes, I know I said I would take it easy, but Lucy had a friend that's returning from abroad and wanted a little Christmas cash. She came in last week, and she was really good, so we are giving her a trial next week. Lucy is going to supervise as I'm having the week off, I'm back to work next Monday." Tristan seems placated with that.

"Ok. Are you taking Danny with you?" He asks. Our new bodyguard and driver since…since what happened left us without one.

"Tristan, its Saturday. Danny has the weekends off, remember?" I remind him.

He frowns down at me. "But I thought that was only when you weren't going anywhere?"

I can't help rolling my eyes at him. "Tristan, I am not having this discussion again. I didn't know I was going to be going out, it's a last minute decision. Besides, I'm perfectly safe," I tell him in my most assuring voice.

He sighs heavily. "Alright, you'll have your mobile with you?" He asks.

"Yes, I have my mobile," I reply, trying not to get worked up about the fact that he's being overprotective again – I know it's because he loves me so much.

"Is it fully charged?" He asks, his chocolate brown eyes distracting me from my mission.

"Yes, my darling. And I have the emergency PAYG mobile, safely tucked away." I say.

"Good, are you sure I can't tempt you to eat anything?" he asks again.

I narrow my eyes at him, so he raises his hands in the air in full surrender. I turn feeling a little annoyed, and head out of his office, leaving the door wide open behind me.

"How about a cup of tea?" he asks, as he follows me out.

"I'm not thirsty," I tell him, smiling now, because I know that's his way of getting me to the breakfast bar so he *can* tempt me with something.

"Ok – Edith!" Tristan shouts as he continues to follow me, 'poached eggs on toast please," he says.

I cock an eyebrow up at him. "You should have some wilted spinach with that or some asparagus," I tell him because I care about him. And he doesn't always eat enough greens.

"With wilted spinach *and* asparagus," he shouts to Edith, with an added chuckle.

I try to hide my smile. "You know it's her day off, don't you!" I tell him.

He throws his cute, innocent, big wide-eyed puppy dog smile at me, and it has the desired effect. I practically melt, and a strange fluttering spreads throughout my body. And I'm reminded again of how much I love him, and how much deeper our love has grown. If it keeps doing this every year, getting deeper I mean, it may wipe me out and crush me under the power of it – I shake my head at that silly thought.

"Edith doesn't mind, she told me so earlier," Tristan adds, a little smugly.

I shake my head at him again and head over to the utility room, with Tristan following. I pick up my winter coat, which Tristan takes from me, and ever the gentleman, he helps me slip my arms in. He turns me then, his face now serious, and begins buttoning me up.

"Why don't you wait a couple of hours and I can come with you?" he says. "I'd feel a lot happier," he quickly adds.

I sigh inwardly, knowing my baby will always worry, it's in his nature. I grab my over the shoulder bag with my keys, mobiles and wallet, and pull it over my head, so it rests on my hip.

"Got everything?" he asks. I nod once. "Darling, are you sure you're ok?" he asks, his fingers tipping my chin back, so I have to look up at him – And I know he means about the moment I just had.

"Yes," I whisper back, and not wanting to get into a deep discussion about my safety, or what just happened, I reach up and kiss his soft, full lips. "See you later sexy pants!" I tease. He grins broadly hearing me say that, and I give him a quick wave as I head out the front door.

Under the large porch, I take a moment to compose myself. Almost losing Tristan that day has really taken its toll on me, and some blurry vision part of it keeps trying to come back as I sleep, but thankfully George and Cindy have been helping me with that. Still feeling a little off balance, I take a deep breath and blow out the memory, it's a *'letting it go'* technique that Cindy, my hypnotherapist taught me.

I do this several times, and within minutes, I am back to my normal self, well, as normal as I can be. Which just proves how much better I am doing, because something like that would have left me shaken for the rest of the day. Again, I think it's down to Tristan, and how safe and settled I feel with him, there really is something special about marriage, and knowing that person will always be there for you, and that you are now life partners, in it together forever.

I smile widely at that thought and look up at the sky. There's no sign of this damn awful rain relinquishing. So bracing myself for the cold, I take a deep breath and dash through the rain, towards my new car that automatically unlocks as I reach it, well,…it's not really a car. Despite the fact that I love Tristan's F-Type, I decided when Tristan was adamant I have my own car, that I wanted a 4x4. My reason for this is that we are now Godparents, and I wanted something that was going to be easy to get baby Mei, and Lily, in and out of when we are babysitting them. And whenever I have Mei, Lily comes too, she loves her 'little sister' as she calls her. And yes, I have become the aunty I should have always been to Lily, I guess you could say I'm making up for lost time.

Anyway, Tristan didn't seem too impressed with the choice of car that I wanted, but a week later I came home to find a brand new Range Rover Sport sitting in the driveway, and of course, it was the top model. It' an Automatic, 5.0 litre, Supercharged, V8, 4WD model in Aintree Green, which is a deep green colour - that part Tristan got right.

But as for the rest, she's a beast; in-fact that's what I've named her 'The Beast' - You should hear the noise it makes when you press the engine on button, and the sound of the engine revving is shocking. It actually startled Mei the first time she was in the back. I had to quickly sing a song from the Lion King to calm her down – *Ugh! It's ridiculous!*

Tristan's answer to the fact that he got me such a brutal model was that it's the best one in the range, and he wanted the reassurance that if I had a problem, the car would get me home safely. Which is a little crazy considering I only have a ten-minute drive to work, or Robs, or Gladys'; and it's only a thirty-minute drive to Debs.

Opening the door, I jump inside, my hair already wet from the rain, and fire her up. She growls to life, actually making me jump a little. But I have to admit, I love the fact that all my tunes are in her database, and all I have to do is press play. Then remembering to call Gladys, I use the controls on the screen – as my mobile automatically connects – and hit the call button, it only rings a couple of times then it's answered by Malcolm.

"Hi, dad!" I say, feeling excited to see them both.

"Hello darling, how are you?" He asks, he sounds happy.

"I'm great thanks, you?" I sound happy too – I think I'm finally getting used to it.

"Very well thank you Coral, are you calling for your mom?" He asks.

"Actually, I was going to ask if I can pop over?" I say.

"Of course darling," I can hear his smile.

"Ok, see you in ten," I say.

"Lovely, see you then," Malcolm replies.

I press the end call button, and pulling forward, with the engine grumbling beneath me, I head out the driveway. The music continues on a shuffle - Big Brovaz's Baby Boy starts playing. So using the steering wheel controls, I turn it up loud, because it's become my favourite song for Tristan and me, it's like it was written for us. As I sing away, feeling happy and excited for the coming day, I head out towards Gladys and Malcolm's new pad, which happens to be on the Marina.

I am sure they bought this particular swanky four bedroom townhouse, located in a private mews, in the most exclusive part of the Marina, because the golf course is only five minutes away – and Malcolm sure loves playing golf. But also for the fact that it has enough bedrooms to host Malcolm's daughters, their husbands and kids when they come to stay, which is quite often. And it's only a five-minute walk away from Bob, which has helped to put my mind at rest about him being down there on his own.

Although I really do miss seeing him every day, taking care of him, and making sure he's eating well, I am relaxed about it, because Gladys has taken over. She goes on walks with him every day, does his grocery shopping, and a couple of weeks ago, when a really bad storm came in overnight, Gladys and Malcolm got him over to their place, and he stayed the night. So all in all, things are going really well, and somehow, we have become this bigger family, that's full of fun and love, and good times.

ARRIVING AT THE private gates, I press the button for access, and I'm buzzed in. Carefully crawling the beast forward I pull up outside their house and park in the designated bay. Gladys swings the front door open and comes dashing out towards me. I smile and wave to her as I kill the engine, grab my bag, and step outside into her warm arms that squeeze me tightly.

"Oh Coral,' she gushes, 'you look so happy darling," she adds, kissing my cheek several times, but taking no notice of the fact that we are getting soaked out in the rain.

I giggle at her. "I am," I say, trying to shield my face from the cold rain.

"Oh, goodness!' Gladys says, 'raining cats and dogs again," she adds as we dash inside.

I quickly strip my coat, hang it up to dry, and turn to Gladys. "You look happy to mom," I say, and pull her in for another hug. It's so nice feeling like this now, to be able to fully appreciate my family and love them without hesitation or fear of being rejected somehow.

"Yes, very happy," she whispers, and I can tell she's been crying. I'm about to ask her why, when I hear it playing in the background – It's A Wonderful Life – It always gets to Gladys, and makes her feel weepy and sentimental.

"Mom," I chuckle, 'why do you do it to yourself? You know it makes you sad," I add.

"Do what?" she asks, dabbing her tears.

"It's A Wonderful Life?" I say – and I get it, it's a really lovely film, and every time it makes me cry at the end, but Gladys really blubbers at it, from beginning to end.

"Oh pish-posh," she says, waving her hanky at me. I shake my head and laugh at her, and then I notice Malcolm walking down the hallway with a big smile on his face.

"Dad!" I gush and step into his arms for a hug. I have absolutely no bad feelings when I hug Malcolm, I only feel love - It's a revelation!

"How are you darling?" He asks as he gives me a little squeeze of his own.

"I'm really great," I say, pulling back to look up at him, we give each other a kiss on the cheek, which makes Gladys make a funny squeaky noise – she still gets very emotional about everything that happened, and she's been watching *that* film! Malcolm and I both turn to look at her, she's fighting back the tears again, I can tell. I want to roll my eyes at her, but I don't.

"Cup of tea?" Malcolm asks, obviously not wanting to make a big deal out of it.

"Love one," I reply, he releases me and heads down the hallway towards the kitchen. I turn to Gladys and shake my head at her. "Oh mom, what are you like?" I say in a soft voice as I wrap my arm around her waist, and lean my head on her shoulder.

"Oh Coral," she sniffs, placing her arm around my waist too, 'life has changed so much, for you, and for me. I never thought we'd be this happy," she adds, not surprising me, because of her watching *that* film.

"I know," I whisper, with a little laugh as we begin walking down the hallway.

"Bob was here last night," Gladys says in a lighter voice.

"Yeah...was he ok?" I ask.

"He's got a little bit of a cold at the moment, but I took him to the doctors, and they checked him out. No infections or temperature so he's not on antibiotics, he just needs to keep warm and dry. I've been taking him my chicken stew every day to keep his energy levels up."

I stop walking, my face falling at this news. "Why didn't you tell me?" I whisper, wishing she had. I would have had him come and stay with us.

"He didn't want to worry you," Gladys says then she hesitates, frowning slightly.

My heart starts to race. "What? What is it?" I ask, my mouth suddenly feeling bone dry.

Gladys looks down at me and places her hand on my cheek. "He's not getting any younger sweetheart," she softly says. *Oh god, not this again!*

I instantly feel relieved that it's not some new information that I don't know about. You see, this is not the first time Gladys has given me the whole *'Bob won't be around forever'* speech. Which I am well aware of, and I will deal with it the day it comes, but for now, he's fine. I stare back at her, and I know she's going to tell me all over again because she's been watching *that* film.

"I know that mom, you don't need' - "It's just that sometimes, without any warning...people at that age can suddenly' – "Please don't say it, mom!" I interrupt. "It's Christmas!" I add, hoping she'll let it go.

"I know darling. I just want you to prepare yourself for the fact that it may happen,' she says, I try to butt in, but she continues. "When my father died, it happened that way, and as devastating as it is, it's better than suffering. That's the most important thing darling. You wouldn't want Bob to suffer would you?" she softly asks.

I look up at her, my eyes wide, not quite believing we are having this conversation. "No,' I scoff, 'of course not," I say, sighing in defeat. *Please, can we change the subject!*

Gladys squeezes my shoulders. "I don't think it *will* happen,' she soothes then chuckles to herself, 'he's a tough old bugger," she adds. *Holy mother of God! – I love her to bits, but she really picks her timing!*

I can't help shaking my head at her. "You really had to tell me that now - at Christmas!" I say, my voice high pitched.

Gladys seems to realise her blunder. "Oh...I didn't think, well...I'm sorry sweetheart. You're right, it is Christmas, a time to be cheery!" she says, and giggles at herself.

This time I do roll my eyes. "How's Joyce?" I say, then immediately regret asking - I'll probably get some long drawn out speech about how you never know when you're time is up – which is true – but who wants to hear that at this time of year!

"Oh she's doing ok, most importantly she's coping," Gladys replies cheerily, and I feel relieved again. "One day at a time," she adds. I nod my reply. "So what brings you here?" Gladys asks as we enter the kitchen. It's brand new, very modern, and is much larger than the one she's used to, but it suits them both.

As I look through the open plan kitchen to the lounge, I notice they haven't got any Christmas decorations up either, which is odd, Gladys has always had them up on the 1$^{st}$ December. The only thing they have got is a miniature Christmas tree sat on the kitchen table and a few cards up on the wall. *Strange!*

"Can't I pop over without having a reason?" I tease, my eyebrows raised.

"Here you are Coral," Malcolm says as he hands me a cuppa.

"Thanks," I take it off him and warm my hands on the mug.

We all sit around the breakfast table with our mugs of tea. Malcolm was evidently reading his newspaper when I interrupted them, and Gladys was watching *that* film, which she quickly scuttles into the living room to pause, moments later she's back at my side.

As I take another sip of tea, I begin to feel a little warm, so I reach up and remove the chocolate silk scarf that Tristan bought for me, which makes Gladys frown.

"What?" I ask, seeing the look on her face.

"Coral," she scorns, 'you look like skin and bone!"

I suddenly realise that the matching chocolate v-neck jumper I am wearing is showing my collarbone, and admittedly, I am a bit slimmer than I used to be. "Oh, mom..." I mumble, not wanting her on my back like Tristan.

"Are you unwell?" she asks her frown still there.

"No!" I say, exasperated.

"Darling..." Malcolm pipes up. "Coral looks very well, and healthy to me," he says, looking over the brim of his glasses at her. Which makes me start to smile, because he looks like Professor Dumbledore from the Harry Potter movies - which I am now a fan of, courtesy of Lily - with his white hair, and matching short beard. And his look to Gladys says it all. *Thank you Malcolm!*

Gladys purses her lips then seems to gather herself together. "So you just thought you'd pop over and see us?" she asks, as though I haven't done that before.

"Yes, and no," I chuckle. "I wanted to tell you both something," I add.

Malcolm looks as relaxed as ever hearing me say that, but Gladys suddenly squeals, brings her hands to her mouth and starts blubbering. "I can't believe it!" she says, her voice high pitched and gleeful.

Malcolm and I glance at each other, both equally puzzled at Gladys' reaction.

"Mom," I chuckle, 'what are you' – "You're pregnant!" she squeals again. "Oh, darling! That's why you've lost so much weight, that can happen you know," she adds, her voice full of joy and excitement.

I suddenly feel guilty for saying I had something to tell them, and then I think how stupid I *was* for saying that. I know Gladys is desperate to be a Granny again, as she has asked several times when I've seen her *'if there's a bun in the oven yet'* which feels like she's pressuring me, but I am not ready – No way, not yet!

"Mom," I say, placing my hand over hers. "I'm not pregnant," I tell her in the softest voice I can manage.

"Gladys!" Malcolm chuckles, 'every time she opens her mouth to say something you think she's pregnant." He lightly scolds.

"Yes Malcolm, thank you for that," Gladys says, and it's her turn to give him a look that would have shaken me to the core when I was younger.

I giggle at the scenario as they tend to remind me of Tristan and I and how we really do push each other's buttons sometimes, but underneath it all there's pure love.

"Hey you two," I pipe up, 'no arguing please," I add in a funny, light voice.

They look away from one another, but it's Malcolm that turns to me. "What is it you wanted to say Coral?" he asks. Gladys is fidgeting, obviously still unhappy.

I take a breath and begin. "Well, if it's ok with mom, I

wanted to ask if it's you're happy with me hosting Christmas this year?"

I wait for the bombshell to drop, and for their reaction.

# THREE

EVERY YEAR SINCE I have lived with Gladys she has hosted the best Christmases. When we were younger, Debs and I could have our friends over for Christmas Eve, and we were allowed a sneaky glass of wine, then on Christmas Day, John and Joyce would come around and spend the day with us.

As time went by, it became Debs and Scott, Justin, Harriett and I, and always John and Joyce. Then after the whole fiasco with Justin and Harriett, I met Rob, so he and Carlos would always be there Christmas Eve and Christmas Day, along with Bob. And then Lily arrived, and we'd all help with convincing her that Father Christmas was real, and if she behaved herself, he would come down the chimney with her presents.

Gladys was always the best host. No matter how much work she had to do, although Joyce, Debs and I would try to help, she would always look after everyone, making sure they were never hungry and constantly refilling their glasses. And in a way, I don't want to take that away from her, but I really want to do this.

"You,' Gladys laughs, 'host Christmas?"

That reaction does not inspire confidence.

I frown at her. "Thanks for the vote of confidence mom," I can't help being sarcastic.

Malcolm beams widely. "I think that's a lovely idea sweetheart," he says.

I smile shyly at him. "Thanks, Malcolm," I take his free hand, and give it a squeeze, then turn to Gladys. "Mom, I don't want to take anything away from you' – "Away from me? Goodness darling, we didn't think...oh dear," she sighs, looking forlorn.

I frown at her odd behaviour.

"We'll be away this Christmas,' Malcolm tells me, 'we were

actually going to tell everybody next weekend when the family is over for a stay," he adds. That explains the phone call Tristan, and I got last week to invite us over for dinner next Saturday night, which of course we said yes to, and now I know why.

My face falls. "Oh..." I whisper - My Christmas wish is crashing down around my ears.

"Oh sweetheart," Gladys says, and awkwardly pulls me in for a hug. "We're going to the house in Spain. I didn't think it would bother you so much now you have Tristan." Gladys pulls back and places her hands on my shoulders. "It's just, such a lot has happened this year, and we really fancied getting away, just the two of us," Gladys glances at Malcolm, looking guilty.

I take a deep breath, knowing she's right, it has been a crazy year. "Mom, it's fine, really it is. I understand you want to do that," I tell her, smiling widely, though not feeling it inside.

She strokes my cheek. "Really darling, you don't mind?" she asks, her eyes searching for the truth.

I guess it will be everyone else bar Gladys, Malcolm, Joyce... and John. I sigh inwardly but pick myself back up. I don't want them feeling bad about not being here. No way, I've spent too much of my life making others feel bad or guilty because of my weird ways – It's time it came to an end.

I take Gladys' hands in mine, lean forward and kiss her cheek. "Mom, you deserve this. You both do. Every Christmas I have had with you has been wonderful. As I child, I felt the magic of Christmas all around me, even though I had my... problems. And as an adult, you always made it so much fun and made us all feel so warm and welcome. I will treasure those memories for the rest of my life." I smile warmly at her, wanting her to know I really do mean what I'm saying.

"Oh darling," she gushes, pulling me to my feet so she can hug me. She squeezes me so tightly that I'm suffocating against her large breasts. I have to pat her back so she'll release me. "You're sure you don't mind?" she asks again, as she pulls back, allowing me to breathe again.

"No Mom, its fine. But when are you leaving?" I ask, wondering if they can at least have Christmas Eve with us.

"On the 20$^{th}$," Gladys replies. And my heart sinks even further. "Now, I have yours and Tristan's Christmas presents in the cupboard, let me fetch them for you," she says and wobbles away.

I sit back down, pick up my mug of tea and take a sip,

thinking how I better get their presents organised and over to them before they go away.

"Thank you Coral," Malcolm says; his voice sincere.

I look up at him and smile. "Every word I said was true Malcolm, mom is the best host, and she always made Christmas feel so magical."

He leans forward on the table. "No, I mean for being so understanding. Gladys was worried, even though I told her not to be," he whispers, 'she still worries about your reaction to things, to change. But I told her that she needs to let go of the past, of the old you, and embrace the new you," he adds in hushed tones. "You're stronger, happier and more balanced now. Even I can see that, and I haven't known you that long." He winks at me, smiles broadly and leans back against the chair.

I think my chin has hit the floor, so I take a moment to compose myself, and then I reply. "You're right Malcolm, if she'd have said that to me last year, I would have freaked out...' I look down at the floor, feeling guilt-ridden for all the ways in which I made Gladys feel bad. 'She'll never know how sorry I am. If I could turn back time and take it all back, I would." I swallow hard, feeling a little sick at the truth of my own words.

Unexpected tears spring to my eyes – *God damn it!*

Malcolm comes and sits opposite me, takes my free hand and squeezes it tight. "Don't waste your time thinking about the past Coral. It doesn't do any of us any good. It's full of regret, mistakes and what ifs, and I can tell you now, life is far too short for that. It whizzes by whether you are living in the past, present or future, and if you spend too much time thinking about the past before you know it, ten years have gone by, and you have no idea what you did in those years." I gaze at Malcolm, blinking back more tears, wondering if he's referring to himself, and what he went through after his divorce.

He continues. "Look, most of the time your Mom is on cloud nine. She's so happy you have pushed through everything that was holding you back, and that you have Tristan. She loves the new you, she really does. But like any mother, she will always worry about her children's happiness." Malcolm leans forward and plants a swift kiss on my forehead – And my heart overflows with love for him.

Everything he said to me on my wedding day, as we danced together, he has stuck by. Like how he was with me just a few short weeks ago. I'd turned up at the house, pretending I wanted to speak to Gladys, when really I just wanted a breather from

Tristan, as we'd had an argument. Gladys wasn't home, but Malcolm was there. He knew something was up, so he asked, and I said nothing, so he reminded me of what he told me as we danced that day.

I bit the bullet and told him of our argument, and he gave me a different perspective on it, one that helped. He's been a godsend ever since. It's a feeling that I'm still getting used to, having a male role model, a father so to speak, who I know, categorically, will always have open arms, good advice, and be a sounding board for me – I feel very blessed. And I'm so grateful, every day that he's with Gladys, that they are together and no longer lonely.

"Thanks, dad," I whisper a couple of tears bouncing down my cheeks.

We hug again, surprising Gladys as she enters the kitchen.

"Everything ok?" she asks, looking from me to Malcolm.

I sniff and then laugh. "Yeah mom, it's all good," I say, feeling decidedly better for Malcolm's pep talk. "Back in a second," I dash off to the bathroom, and once in there I mop up the tears, blow my nose and touch up my makeup.

Taking a deep breath, and staring back at the new me, I make a decision to keep listening to Malcolm's words, because right now, the old part of me wants to resurface. And I know the emotion is guilt. I can feel it there in the background like I want to curl up into a ball, and cry my eyes out for the hell I put Gladys through – but I have to keep moving forward. No matter how strange and alien it can feel at times.

"You can do this Coral Freeman!" I whisper to my reflection, pulling my shoulders back as I do. My big blue eyes look a little too large in my now slimmer face – Hmm...Maybe everyone is right, and I need to start stuffing my face with cakes and chocolate?

I shake my head at myself – *Diabetes heaven that is!*

Heading out the bathroom, I return to the kitchen, and we all spend another hour or so chatting away. My mind drifts to Tristan several times, I can't help it, I am in love with him, and that's what happens when you fall in love – you go crazy!

HALF AN HOUR later, as I'm stood on the porch saying goodbye to mom, and Malcolm is loading the boot with our Christmas presents, I make another decision, to see not only Bob today, but Rob too, and maybe Debs, although I only saw her a few days ago.

"Bye mom, love you lots," I whisper, hugging her tightly.

Gladys chuckles. "Bye darling, be safe in that thing won't you?" she says.

She hates 'The Beast, she thinks it's far too powerful and told Tristan off when she first found out about it. He finally got to experience her wrath. I must admit, it was quite funny seeing his cheeks flame and his gobsmacked expression. He normally can't do anything wrong in Gladys' eyes, but he buggered up this time.

Malcolm jogs back under the porch, and we hug again. "Bye, dad. See you soon."

"Before Saturday?" He asks.

"Yeah...hopefully," I say – And whether he likes it or not Tristan is coming with me, he can't keep avoiding Gladys forever. I run over to 'The Beast' jump inside, place the flask Gladys gave me with Bob's Chicken Stew on the seat next to me, and shake the rain from my fingers. *Ugh! I hate rainy days!*

Starting her up, I glance out the window, and see Gladys and Malcolm on the porch, Gladys is shaking her head and gesticulating to Malcolm, then she waves at me, and storms back into the house. Malcolm rolls his eyes and smiles widely at me, making me laugh. I wave one last goodbye and slowly drive away, trying to keep the engine as quiet as possible, so as not to wind Gladys up even more.

Five minutes later and I am parked at the gym. I stay in the beast for a moment, taking in my surroundings, and marvelling at the fact that I used to live here and walk across this car park every morning. I look to my left, down at the bright yellow row of buildings, which today look dull and grimy, that'll be all the storms we've been having.

Then I look out in front of me, at sea – it's roaring. I can see white-capped waves right out to the horizon, and the sky above is an ominous grey, reflecting down onto the sea which almost looks like liquid metal. And even though I'm inside the beast, I can hear the ferocity of her waves crashing against the Marina, which makes me shudder inside. *Ugh, I hate winter!*

With that thought in mind, I brace myself for the cold wind lashing my face and the rain soaking me, grab Bob's stew and my bag, then jump out of the car, slam the door shut and run as fast as I possibly can without falling over, towards the concourse. As I do, I hear several seagulls and look up above me, I stop and watch for a moment as they manage to fly in sync with the ferocious winds, gliding effortlessly then hovering for a moment as they look down to the ground for something to eat.

As I continue to stare, a big droplet of rain lands straight in my eye, just as a howling gust of wind almost knocks me over. *Damn it!* I quickly hide my face in my coat and scold myself for doing such a daft thing when it's raining so hard. Then reaching the steps to the concourse, I hurry down them, then start running again towards my old studio, and Bob's place next door.

Tristan, many months ago, advised me to keep my studio and rent it out, I took his advice, and with his help, we found the right company. They only deal with holiday lets on the Marinas and other such properties that are on the water. It's really great as I don't have to worry about a thing. They take care of everything, the rentals, maintenance, and the cleaning etc. And to be fair, it has brought in a nice little profit. So I'm shocked to see the lights on in my old studio as I pass it, as I would have thought it not rentable at this time of year. Shrugging that thought off, I knock on Bob's door. Then I think I should have used my key as he maybe upstairs and - The patio door slides open, halting my thoughts.

"Coral?" His face lights up, I can tell he's surprised.

"Hey Bob," I quickly dash inside and close the patio door behind me. Noticing that his studio smells clean, and it's warm and dry. I turn and look at Bob, a wave of guilt washes over me for leaving him, but I push it aside. "Can I stay a while?" I ask.

Bob laughs. "Of course you can, I'm surprised to see you," he says, holding his hands out for my wet coat.

"Thanks, Bob," I say as he takes it off me and hangs it up. "How are you?" I ask.

"I'm fine, you didn't have to come out in this awful weather to see me," he says.

"I didn't. " I lie. "I was just over at moms, and she asked me to bring your Chicken Stew over," I tell him.

"Oh, well that's not so bad then," Bob says.

I place my hand on my hip. "Bob! I would risk hell and high water to come and see you, so please don't say things like that." I say, hoping it came out the right way.

Bob looks guiltily at me, but then I notice something, he's moving a little slower than he normally would, and seems to struggle as he lowers himself onto the sofa.

"Take a pew," he says, patting the spot next to him.

"Have you eaten today Bob?" I softly ask.

"I've had some porridge," he tells me - That would have been at about 6am I imagine.

"Time for some stew then," I say.

"I am hungry," Bob replies.

I head over to the kitchenette, and finding a bowl, I empty the contents of the flask into it so it can cool a little. Then picking up Bob's table, I unfold the legs and place it in front of him. The radio is playing Christmas songs in the background – Cliff Richards' Mistletoe and Wine - and I notice he has a paperback sat next to him.

"Are you hungry enough for a bread roll too?" I ask.

"Sounds good," he says, and as I'm up close to him, I can see he looks a little tired and worn out, which just plays on my fears – I wish Gladys hadn't said that to me. *Ugh!*

Trying to ignore my own thoughts, I find a fresh granary roll, glad that Gladys has recently been shopping, cut it open and smear it with butter. Placing it down in front of Bob, he grumbles up at me.

"I always liked those white rolls you used to get me. Gladys says they are no good for you, but they taste great dipped in soup," he says, and starts digging in.

"Yeah...they are the best tasting Bob, but Gladys is right, they are not as good for you as the Granary," I say.

While Bob eats his stew, I wash the couple of cups that are in the sink, and the flask. When he's done, I do the same with his bowl and plate, all the while, trying not to think about the fact that I'm not here for him every day, not anymore. *Coral, chillax, it's Christmas!*

I shake my head at my wayward thoughts, and once I've folded his table back up and stowed it away, I head back over to Bob and take a seat next to him. "Now, I'm afraid I'm going to have to tell you off Bob," I say.

He smiles widely at me. "Really," he says, wiggling his eyebrows at me.

"Bob! You are such a card. I bet you were a right tear away in your teens," I can't help laughing.

He smiles wistfully at me. "Ladies Man," he corrects.

"Yes, I'm sure you were," I reproach, my tone playful. "Anyway, I'm telling you off because Gladys said you have a cold, and you didn't call me Bob. You promised me you would." I stare at him, eyes wide, waiting to hear his reasons why.

"Well hell...I don't want to disturb you every time something happens," he tells me.

"Every time?" I question, wondering what else has gone on that I don't know about.

Bob looks away, his expression one of guilt.

"Bob...?" I probe, wanting to know what that look is for.

He turns and looks at me with guilty eyes, I swallow hard.

"I fell over," he tells me.

"When?" I whisper, taking his hand in mine.

"Yesterday, after Gladys left," he says, his hand shaking slightly.

I take a deep breath. "Where did you fall, Bob?" I ask.

"Here," he says. "I was tired, it was around six, I was taking my bowl back over to the sink, I felt a little dizzy, and then boom, the next thing I know I'm on the floor. I hurt my hand," he says, and holding it up I see a small bluish-purple bruise where he's evidently tried to save himself. *Holy fuck!*

I take a deep breath, trying to not to freak out about it.

"Luckily that nice young man that's been staying at your place came over. He said he heard a noise, he helped me up, and got me a glass of water," Bob smiles widely at me. "I can see your worry Coral, but please don't. It's not the first time I've fallen over, and I'm fine now. I'll tell you what I told Gladys, I'm tougher than I look."

I look down at the floor, wondering how to approach this. "Please come and stay with me," I whisper.

"No Coral, I'm not doing that. If it makes you feel any better, I'll see the doctor again on Monday." He retorts.

I swallow hard. "Yes, that would make me feel better," I say.

"Then I will go," he replies, rolling his eyes at me. "Everybody has their off days Coral," he adds.

"I know," I whisper, 'I just don't like...not knowing you're ok. And I miss you," I tell him. "I miss our little chats."

He leans in and kisses my cheek. "I miss our little chats too," he says, looking a lot perkier.

I decide being gloomy is not going to make him feel better, or me. "Ok then, how about a game of checkers?" I ask.

"Sounds great," Bob says, his blue eyes lighting up, which relaxes me a little.

I decide staying another hour should give me enough time to assess what he's really like, and if I make the decision that he needs looking at, I'm taking him to the hospital – tonight. We can use my private medical care, and I'll pay for it, whatever the cost. I want him taken care of.

## A Christmas Wish

AN HOUR AND a half pass, and I come to the conclusion that Bob actually is ok. He's sleeping on the sofa at the moment, as he said his knee is hurting him since the fall, and it's making it difficult to get up and down the stairs. I'm definitely taking him to see my private doctor on Monday, Dr Andrews - although he should be called Dr Reeves because he looks a lot like Keanu Reeves - but other than that, thankfully Bob seems in fine spirits.

"Right then Bob," I say as I get to my feet and put on my coat. "Enjoy your roast dinner with Gladys tomorrow, and I'll see you on Monday to take you to my doctors."

"I can see *my* doctor," he says.

"Bob, they probably won't be able to get you in so soon. And I know Dr Andrews will see you for a quick checkup as a favour to me." He's seen me several times during my recovery.

Bob raises his eyebrows and then laughs.

"Ok...ok, so I'm using the fact that he thinks I'm attractive to my advantage," I say, my hands held up in the air.

"I wouldn't let your fella hear you say that," Bob chortles.

"Oh haha, Bob!" I reply, chuckling slightly - then I suddenly remember my plan, my Christmas wish. "Oh yeah, I just remembered, would you like to spend Christmas at my place this year? Gladys is off to sunny Spain with Malcolm. Can you believe it?" I laugh.

"I'll be there Christmas Day, but not Christmas Eve," Bob tells me.

"Oh...why not?" I ask.

"Too noisy," he replies, 'and you know I'm in bed by 9pm," he adds.

I smile warmly at him. "Ok, just Christmas Day then."

Bob smiles back at me then goes to stand.

"No Bob, but you stay there. I'll lock the door behind me," I say, then leaning down I give his cheek a kiss, and hug him gently.

"Thanks, sweetheart," he says, patting my arm. "It was really nice to see you."

"You too Bob," I whisper, trying not to choke up. "See you Monday," I add, and quickly turn away before I start crying.

Then, taking a deep breath, so the cold doesn't shock me so much, I pull the patio door open, step outside and quickly close it behind me. Then I realise I should have got my keys out first, as my hands are already starting to freeze. *Stupid Coral!*

Shaking my head at myself, I finally find them at the bottom of my bag, my hands so cold now I can hardly *feel* the keys, and lock his door. With a quick wave, I turn away ready to dash towards the car, but something stops me, and before I know it, I'm knocking on the patio door to my old studio, about to disturb a complete stranger – *Coral, what are you doing?*

As I stand there, freezing my ass off and hopping from foot to foot to try and keep warm, I wonder if there actually *is* anybody home. Deciding there isn't, as nobody has come to the door, and wanting to get back to the warmth of the beast, I quickly turn, about to run again and slam into a man's chest – *Fuck, that hurt!*

I look up, my nose feeling slightly bruised, and see a pair of eyes I used to love and know. "Holy crap!... Justin?" I squeak, blinking against the rain.

"Hi Coral, are you ok?" He asks; his face dead serious.

"No," I say, the wind whipping my hair around my face, and freezing my exposed earlobes – *What is he doing here?*

In answer to my question, Justin steps forward and unlocks my studio. In stunned silence, I look up at him. "Yes,' he says, 'I'm living here. Come on in out of the rain," he adds and slides the door open. I gawp at him, trying to work out of it's the right thing to do. The rain is lashing against my face, the wind getting into places it shouldn't, and I'm getting colder by the second.

"Coral, get inside before you freeze to death," he says. "I know how you hate the cold," he adds. He's right, I do hate the cold.

As I think that, I feel my teeth start to chatter against one another, my legs feel like blocks of ice, and it feels like I have icicles hanging down from my nostrils. I look up at Justin, then behind him to the warmth of the studio. I want to get inside, out if the icy rain still pelting down on me - *This is a bad idea Coral, don't do it!*

# FOUR

IGNORING MY OWN thoughts, I step into my old studio, which looks completely different due to the makeover it's had, and then Justin slides the door shut. I turn and stare at him, dumbfounded.

"I guess as you are the owner, you have the right to know why I'm here," he says.

I shake my head, feeling a weird shyness that I used to have around him. "I don't have that right," I say, it's almost a whisper.

And I feel myself start to defrost now I'm out of the elements, the feeling in my legs is coming back to me, and my teeth are no longer chattering, but I keep my hands in my coat pockets, as they still feel cold.

He stares back at me, then smiles. "Ok, so...why were you knocking on the door?"

I look up at him again but quickly look away to the wall. "Um...yeah I was wasn't I,' I say, feeling nervous. Justin takes a step towards me, so I take a step back, not wanting any contact.

He holds his hands up. "I was just gonna put the kettle on," he says.

I turn and see I'm almost backed up against the kitchenette, so I quickly step out of his way. "Sorry," I murmur.

He laughs to himself. "You know...I always remember you saying that a lot."

I think I'm still in shock.

"Saying what?" I ask, but I'm distracted by the fact that I'm back in my studio. I can't help looking around the small space, so many memories. Not all good. I get a flashback of finding Bob after Susannah attacked him, I look down at the floor remembering the massive blood stain that was left once the ambulance took Bob away – which is now gone, as it should be, considering it's being rented out.

Justin laughs again, bringing me back to the now. "Tea?" he asks.

I frown at him. "No thanks." I shake my head slightly, trying to stop the old memories of Bob from running, and get back to the now the present, and I suddenly find an inner confidence from somewhere.

"What did I always say?" I ask.

He smiles again, as though he's remembering. "You used to say *'sorry'* all the time. Don't you remember it driving me mad?" I suddenly think of Tristan, and his patience with the fact that I do say it a lot, yet he doesn't lose his temper with me like Justin used to.

I nod my head. "Yes, I do," I reply.

"Sure you don't want' – "I was knocking on your door...my door,' I start to get flustered, as he's turned his gaze on me like he used to. I take a deep breath to calm myself. 'You helped Bob out, my next door neighbour?"

He laughs again. "Don't you mean *'my'* next door neighbour?" *Ugh!* He hasn't changed, everything was always a fucking joke to him - And Bob isn't a joke, he better get that.

I narrow my eyes at him. "Look, I just wanted to say thank you to whoever it was. Bob's supposed to call me if he gets into trouble," I firmly say.

"Well, why don't you give *me* your number, and I'll call you directly... if anything should happen," he says. *Nice try!*

"What are you doing here Justin?" I ask although I have no right to, but I am intrigued.

He sighs and starts drying teacups with a tea-towel. "My flat is being renovated, so I needed somewhere cheap for a few months, the agency made me a four-month deal over the winter months. *Apparently,* they cleared it with the owners," he says, his eyebrows raised.

And I know *he* knows I didn't know about any four-month deal – not that it matters.

"I don't handle any of our properties, Tristan does," I tell him.

He laughs again. "Ooh...our properties." He says.

I note a little jealousy in his tone but ignore it. "So you've finally bought your own place?" I say.

He nods; his face serious. "When I found out you'd got married, I figured you really had moved on, so I thought it was about time I did the same," he says, and now he sounds sad.

"Oh..." I whisper. "And have you...met someone?" I ask, not really knowing if I should be asking that question.

He's still serious. "Not yet, kind of hard to meet someone when you keep comparing them to the girl that you loved and lost," he says.

I freeze. *Is he talking about me?*

He stops drying cups, leans against the kitchenette, and crosses his arms. "You know I mean you, don't you Coral."

I look down to the floor. "It doesn't really matter whether it is me or not Justin," I whisper.

"Doesn't it?" He replies.

I frown at his words. "You cheated on me," I say, wincing slightly at the memory.

"You know, people do make mistakes Coral' – "And I may have forgiven you, had it not been with Harriett," I interrupt, realising that I'm staying pretty calm considering I'm alone with him – I guess I really am changing.

He frowns deeply. "Biggest mistake of my life," he murmurs.

I swallow hard. "I don't want you to be unhappy Justin," I whisper because I don't.

"Then make me happy," he says, looking all wounded and heartbroken, his blue eyes wide as he stares back at me. I realise at that moment that I'm actually feeling sorry for the guy that broke my heart by cheating on me with my best friend, which is ridiculous.

"I'll never leave Tristan – ever. So do yourself a favour Justin, and let it go." I tell him firmly.

He winces. "Harsh words Coral."

I cock my head to the side. "Sometimes the truth hurts," I say with a shrug.

"You've changed," he says.

"You mean I'm not bending to your every will," I state, a little sarcasm coming through.

He smiles at that answer and starts walking over to me.

"Justin..." I warn, getting ready to knee him in the bollocks if he does anything.

"I'm not going to hurt you," he says, and reaching me, he gently pulls my right hand out of my pocket, and holds it tight in his. I instantly notice how I have no reaction, not like I do when Tristan takes my hand.

"You always did have cold hands," he says, smiling at the memory, and I know I should be yanking my hand out of his, but for some unknown reason, I feel it's ok, that it's all innocent.

He continues. "I am so sorry for what I did Coral. I wish I could take it back, but I can't.' He sighs heavily, my hand still in his. "Are you happy?" he asks.

I fervently nod my head and begin to smile. Just thinking about Tristan does that to me. "Yes," I whisper. "I'm very happy," I add.

His eyes close for a moment as he sighs heavily in defeat. "Really happy?" he asks, eyes still closed.

"In a way, I would have never thought possible Justin," I softly tell him.

His eyes open, and I freeze as he looks down at me. "Then I'm happy too," he says, and lightly kisses my cheek. "You deserve all the happiness in the world," he whispers in my ear.

Tears bubble up to the surface. "Justin..." I croak, 'you're making me feel bad," I sniff.

"Sorry," he smiles, standing up straight, releasing my hand as he does – and the joke is not lost on me. I can't help smiling at him, he reciprocates, and then we both start laughing with one another.

I sigh in a weird happy, sad kind of way. "Are you going home for Christmas?" I ask.

He shakes his head. "Mom's moved to Canada, she met some guy online, and that was that." I cock one eyebrow up – Justin's Mom was always, well, in my opinion, a bit of a tart. In all the time I knew Justin, she'd slept with more men than she'd had hot dinners.

"And Kim?" I ask his sister, who's ended up like her mother – five kids, all with different dads. It was always mayhem at her house whenever Justin and I visited – we never stayed long.

"I've had an invite, but I doubt I'll go," he says.

I frown up at him. "So...what are you going to do?" I ask.

"You remember Neil?" he asks.

"Yeah..." I smile up at him – his best friend Neil, very funny, always had us both laughing with the stories he used to tell, and the trouble he would get into, but somehow he'd always wriggle out of it.

"Well, believe it or not, he got married," he says.

My mouth pops open. "The permanent bachelor *'I'm never getting married'* Neil has gone and done it?" I laugh, feeling an ease that used to be between us.

Justin laughs along with me. "Yep, and he's got it bad, but to be fair, his wife Nikki is a pretty cool chick," he says.

"So is that where you're going?" I ask, still laughing slightly.

"Concerned about my well being are you?" He teases.

My face falls. "Justin," I warn.

"I'm teasing – Yes, there's a whole bunch of us so it should be a laugh," he says.

Relief floods through me, knowing he won't be alone, which is what I thought he was about to say, and god knows what I would have done then – probably something stupid like inviting him over for dinner, and that would have gone down like a lead balloon.

Come to think of it, what am I doing right now? I need to leave, this is feeling far too comfortable, and I mean I know, I get it, when you act maturely and respectfully, exes can be in the same room and have a nice conversation, but I also think that once attraction has been there, it never goes away.

"Well, I better get going. Thanks for the offer of tea, and looking after Bob," I say.

"No problem, and all joking aside, you can leave me your number, and I will call if something happens." This time I can tell he's being genuine, but I still think it's dangerous to give him my number. I wouldn't like it if Tristan gave his out to an ex, and just as I think that I have a light bulb moment.

"How about this, I give you the house landline. Someone is always there, and they can get a message to me," I say, and it's not the same as having direct contact with me.

"Sure," Justin pulls his mobile out his pocket, and types in the number I reel off.

I look up at him, lean up onto my tip-toes and kiss his cheek. "Thanks, Justin, Merry Christmas."

He smiles down at me. "Merry Christmas Coral."

We both head over to the door at the same time, which feels odd. "Were you happy living here Coral?" he asks.

I look up at him. "Yeah, most of the time I was…it's pretty cool in the summer," I drift off, wondering about Tristan and I moving again. Being back here has made me realise how much I have missed the smell of the sea, the sound of the seagulls, and the sound of the water lapping against the studio, it's very relaxing.

We smile at one another again, for a little bit longer than we should, I need to break the connection. "Well, see you, Justin," I say and reach out to open the door.

He steps forward, which is very unlike him and pulls it open for me. "I'm learning," he laughs.

And I come to the startling conclusion that Justin has

potential – not for me – but for someone else. Because, if there's one thing I've learned in life, it's that people tend to mimic their parents, and all he ever saw growing up was men treating his mother like crap, and she let them, he never had a male role model to teach him how to behave respectfully towards women.

"It's a step in the right direction," I laugh back. "See ya," I add.

Justin smiles, but I can tell it's forced. "See you Coral."

I step out into the wind and the rain, and as I walk away, I turn back once to wave at him. His face is solemn, but then he half smiles, his hand held up, and I continue onwards in the knowledge that somehow, that was meant to be, and that I feel even freer than I did before that conversation happened. I pull my coat tighter around me as run back towards the car park, hoping that at some point in the future, Justin finds the kind of happiness I have.

AS I DRIVE ACROSS town towards Rob's pad, I can't help going over how strange that was with Justin and then wondering if I should tell Tristan. I wasn't like anything happened, or ever will happen. But I get the feeling that if I don't share this with him, it may come back and bite me on the ass, which could cause him to think I had something to hide, which I don't. Rolling my eyes at my overthinking, I try to get back to my Christmas wish. *Ok, concentrate Coral!*

So far, we have Bob coming over, and that's it. And to be fair, he'll probably do as he normally does, eat Christmas Dinner, then snooze the afternoon away, which is fine, I don't mind that at all, whatever makes him happy, but it's not like there's going to be lots of fun and games going on.

I sigh inwardly, and then I think of Danny, and I realise I'm not actually sure what he's doing either. Probably spending Christmas with Joe, as they are now an item; well, more than an item actually. They have fallen deeply in love, I hear wedding bells a-ringing, I'm so pleased for them both. And Danny is proving day by day that he is a wonderful father to Joe's kids, so I decide to invite him, and Joe and her kids, as I don't want anyone to feel left out, especially Danny with everything he's been through.

As I park the beast at Rob & Carlos' pad, I say a quick prayer, hoping they say yes to my invite, then grab my bag and jump out of the car, eager to see them. I have really missed having just me and Rob time, and also time with Carlos too, but that's what happens when you become parents. You can't get out and about as much as you used to, which in a way is like having a sense of freedom taken away.

But those are my worries, not Rob and Carlos'. If anything, they are revelling in it, and have proven to be amazing, patient, caring, and very loving parents. And maybe my invite will help take the pressure off them for the day? They can come over, have a lovely meal, and just relax and enjoy the day.

The elevator pings, letting me know I have reached their floor. I skip towards their front door, and once there I press the doorbell, instantly regretting it as I hear baby Mei cry out at the noise – *Shit! I'm supposed to text Rob or Carlos first in-case she's asleep – Double crap!*

I'm definitely in trouble. Rob opens the door, looking happy but knackered. "Hi," he says, with a warm but tired smile on his face.

"I'm so sorry," I whisper, feeling guilty as hell. "I forgot to text!"

Rob starts chuckling at me. "Look at your face!" Evidently, he is finding my expression amusing.

"Hey!" I protest.

"She's not asleep," he chuckles, ushering me inside, and then pulling me in for a kiss and a hug.

"But I heard her cry," I whisper.

"Yeah..." he laughs, "because Carlos is trying to feed her pureed vegetables!"

"Well, at least he's trying to feed her something that's good for her!" I retort.

"Would you want to eat pureed vegetables?" he snorts.

"No, maybe not," I chuckle, "but he may have more luck if he adds some fruit," I add as an afterthought. I'm sure Debs used to do that with Lily.

"Well, you can tell Carlos that!" Rob laughs. "I've been watching this charade for almost half an hour. I keep telling him she doesn't like it, and he should just quit. But will he listen to me? Oh no, Carlos knows best!" Rob snorts sarcastically.

"Glad to see you are being so helpful and supportive to Carlos in this endeavour," I reply dryly, which just makes Rob laugh even harder. *Poor Carlos!*

I shake my head at him and follow him into the kitchen, only to find Carlos sat on a chair that's facing baby Mei, who's in a high-chair, with a not so happy look on his face. I double take as I realise Carlos' face is splattered with green slop, and it's all down his t-shirt too.

Mei is giggling in delight.

"Kodak moment!" Rob laughs as he pulls out his mobile and takes the shot.

This makes Carlos glare at Rob. "It is not funny Rob!" He growls, but he can't help smiling.

"Hey Carlos," I chuckle.

"Hello sunshine," Carlos replies. "What brings you here?"

"Christmas!" I reply excitedly, and walk over and kiss him on top of his head, then do the same to Mei.

"God...don't remind me," he says.

"What? Not looking forward to it this year?" I ask.

"I just want to sleep through it, to be honest with you," he wearily says. "Parenting is hard work, and very tiring." He turns to Mei, leans forward and kisses her chubby cheek. "But so worth it," he adds with an unconditional look of love in his eyes. Then he tries to spoon feed her more green goop, but Mei is turning her face away in disgust.

"Try adding a banana Carlos, Debs used to do that," I pipe up, suddenly remembering her saying that Bananas are a mom's best friend, which I didn't get at the time. *Now I understand!*

"Really?" Without another word, he gets to his feet, adds what's left of the pureed vegetables to the blender, peels a banana, and purees it up. Within a couple of minutes, he's sat in front of Mei again.

"Ok little one, let's try this one more time." Adding a little puree to the spoon, he does the classic train coming into the station routine that parents tend to do so that it's a game, and hopefully, the baby will eat the slop. Mei gobbles down the first spoonful without a fight and then thrashes her arms and legs about in joy.

"Oh my God!" Carlos seems shocked but quickly regains his composure. "Ok...ok...let's see if we can finish the whole bowl." With more choo-choo noises he continues to feed Mei without any further splattering or complaint from her.

"Coral Freeman you are a Godsend," Carlos tells me as he feeds her the last spoonful. "Want a job as a Nanny?" He chuckles.

I smile at him but ignore that one. I'm still debating on whether or not I'll make a good mother. The thought terrifies me if I'm honest. And now I've gone and promised Tristan that at some point in the future we will have all of this to contend with. Then I think back to the look on Gladys' face earlier today, and I feel guilty again for some reason, that I haven't provided her with a grandchild.

I quickly quash those thoughts and smile warmly at Carlos as he cleans Mei's fingers and face, then his face and t-shirt. I watch Mei reach her arms out to Carlos, scrunching her little fingers together. Carlos picks Mei up, and she stares adoringly up at him as he gently rocks her, she then yawns widely, and I watch in adoration as she falls safely asleep in his arms.

"I'll just go and put her down," Carlos whispers.

I turn to Rob who's watching Carlos walk down the hallway. "You just can't keep your eyes off him, can you?" I can't help teasing.

Rob turns to me, eyes filled with tears, taking me by complete surprise. "She's just such a joy, such a happy little girl." He says, sniffing once.

"Oh," I whisper, he's never been this honest about Mei before.

"I thought it would be horrendous Coral, ' he says, keeping his voice low, 'crying and poopie nappies and no sleep, admittedly we don't get as much sleep as we used to, but I never thought it would be like this. She mostly sleeps through the night, she rarely cries, and she laughs so much, 'tis a joy to behold," he tells me, his eyes shining brightly with love and happiness.

"Oh Rob, I'm so pleased for you both. And maybe she's so happy because she's picking up on the fact that you and Carlos are so happy? You know...she can feel it, so it makes her feel... happy and secure?"

Rob takes the couple of steps needed and crushes me into his arms. "You may be right sunshine."

I laugh at him, pull back and stare up at my best friend. "Happy?"

"Very happy," he replies. "And you - How are things with the hunk?" Rob has taken to calling Tristan that name when it's just us. And I think it's because he knows it winds me up.

"Rob!" I scold.

"What?" he laughs innocently.

"You know I don't like that," I playfully tell him.

"Yeah right,' he retorts, 'you know he is one, so why bother challenging it?" *Ugh!*

I lightly punch his arm for good measure. "He's fine, and I'm fine and...well,' I take a deep breath, 'I wanted to invite you all over for Christmas."

"Aren't you going around to Gladys'? Actually, come to think of it, we haven't had our invite yet?" He says his brows pulled together, completely ignoring my invite, but as I take a closer look, I'd say he looks a little preoccupied.

"Well no, and I don't think you'll get one this year as she is spending Christmas shacked up in sunny Spain with Malcolm!" I tell him, with crossed arms – *Ok, so I'm a little peeved about it.*

"Yeah right..." Rob laughs. Not believing a word I am saying.

"Rob, I'm dead serious," I retort.

"Oh! You-are-kidding-me!" He squeaks, enunciating each word. "What about us?" he adds. I start laughing at his pissed off expression. He is not a happy bunny.

"Rob!" I laugh. *Definitely did not hear my invite for the day!*

"Oh! This is not happening! What about her famous Christmas dinner, she always gets everything spot on!' He says, his hands are being thrown about as he rages, I want to interrupt him, but I decide to let him vent it all out. "And what about her Christmas pudding, and homemade brandy sauce?...Oh!...And what about the mince pies? You know they're my favourite!" He stops venting, his nostrils still flaring and looks down at me in utter disgust.

"What?" I frown.

"This is your fault!" he says, his voice rising, 'only reason she's doing this is that you've gone and got shacked up with lover boy!"

"Rob!" I scold, frowning deeply at him for saying that – *Jeez!* "Chill out will you, it's only Christmas dinner!" I add.

"I will not chill out!" he shouts.

I stare, gobsmacked for the second time today, at my best friend.

"I don't believe this!" he shouts again.

I finally find my voice. "Well believe it!" I snap, 'and just, so you know, I was going to invite you all over to have Christmas with Tristan and me, but now you've gone and thrown that in my face, you can stick it where the sun don't shine!" I add, my voice rising automatically as my temper fires up. I turn, feeling thoroughly heartbroken by my friend's words, and head towards the door – *I can't quite believe he just said that to me!*

"What's going on in here?" Carlos hisses as he returns to the living room, and I can tell he's about to tell us both off for shouting.

"Nothing!" I croak, trying to keep the tears at bay. I cross

## A Christmas Wish

my arms, feeling totally pissed at Rob. Carlos stares at us both, crosses *his* arms too, and narrows his eyes at Rob.

"What have you said?" he asks, his tone hushed.

"Ask her," Rob hisses, and crosses his arms.

And at that moment, I don't know why, but I want to laugh. The three of us are all stood there, arms crossed, in a semi-circle, as though we are about to go into battle.

I start to smile.

"I dunno what you're smiling at," Rob huffs.

Which makes me stifle a laugh – And I know I shouldn't be laughing. My best friend just went bonkers at me for something that a, isn't even my fault, and b, I have no control over.

Rob's lips twitch. "Stop laughing," he titters.

Carlos is smiling too, so I look down at the floor, trying to hide the giggle that wants to burst out of me. "Can someone please tell me what's going on?" Carlos says.

I look up at Rob, who huffs grumpily at me. "Gladys is going to Spain for Christmas," I say.

Carlos shrugs his shoulders. "So?"

"So Robs pissed about it, and he seems to think it's all my fault," I hiss, feeling bruised again.

"Rob!" Carlos scolds, 'what's that got to do with Coral?"

Rob seems to deflate like a balloon. "Nothing," he sighs, 'I'm so sorry Coral, I didn't mean what I said, it was such a shock that's all, and I'm grumpy when I'm tired, you know that," I nod, knowing full well it's true. Rob pushes his bottom lip out, he almost looks childlike. "We always go to Gladys' for Christmas' – "I thought we were agreed," Carlos interrupts.

"Well..." Rob replies, 'I hadn't really made my mind up," he adds mulishly, and turns his face away from Carlos – *What's that all about?*

"Rob!" Carlos scolds. He's definitely in trouble with Carlos. *I am not having a good day!*

"Agreed to what?" I ask, looking from Rob to Carlos.

Carlos turns to me. "To stay here this year, you know, stay in, as in no parties, no hangovers – trust me they are not worth it when you have a baby – but now it sounds like I'm the only one that came to the agreement." Carlos sarcastically says, glaring unhappily at Rob.

Rob looks up at the ceiling. "Fine,' he huffs, 'if you want to stay in and be boring..." he lets the sentence linger in the air.

"I'm gonna fall out with you tonight!" Carlos snaps at Rob.

"Wait!" I pipe up, 'are you telling me that you were serious

Carlos and that you guys have no intention of going anywhere this year, whether it was Gladys', or mine?" I ask, narrowing my eyes at Rob.

"Yes, we *mutually,*' Carlos emphasises that part to Rob, 'agreed that we would stay in this year," he states.

"Then why' – I stop, not wanting to get into another argument with Rob. "Ok, so I don't put you guys down for Christmas Eve or Day, right?"

"Correct,' Carlos says, 'but thanks for the invite," he adds.

"You're welcome," I reply. "Well, as that's all sorted, I'll be on my way," I add, wanting to cry again.

*Holy crap!* – What I thought was going to be a lovely day out, minus the weather, seeing family and friends who gladly and happily accept my invitation, has basically turned into a shit storm.

"I'm sorry Coral," Rob whines, his arms held out for a hug. And although I'm still a feeling a little sore, I hug my best friend. "Forgive me?" he whispers in my ear.

"Yes," I sigh, as I kiss his cheek, and then I head for the door.

Carlos is the one that follows me. "God he's a bugger sometimes," Carlos says.

I don't smile, or laugh, I just pull the door open.

"Hey," Carlos stops me, his hand on my shoulder, 'I'm sorry we're not coming Coral."

I shake my head at him. "It's fine, I understand, things are different now. You have Mei," I murmur, and try to leave.

"Then what's wrong?" Carlos asks.

I turn, eyes watering and shake my head.

"Oh come on sunshine," he says and hugs me tightly. "If it means that much to you, we'll come over," he adds.

I sniff loudly. "No Carlos, it's just that...it's going to be so different you know...John is...gone,' I swallow hard, 'Joyce is in Florida, mom and dad are going to Spain, you guys are staying in...' I shake my head again, and pull back from the hug. "I just wanted a big family Christmas, that's all," I say, trying to calm myself down. "I guess...you can't always get what you want in life." *No god damn Christmas Wishes that's for sure!*

Carlos smiles sympathetically at me. "I'm sorry it hasn't worked out for you," he says.

"Yeah...me too, but maybe it's meant to be," I say, feeling a little lighter.

"There are always other things to be grateful for," Carlos says.

I nod in complete agreement and then smile widely. "I guess Tristan and I are going to have a sexy Christmas alone after all," I say, making Carlos chuckle. "Well...that's if everyone else says no," I add with a frown. I decide at that moment to call Debs from the car – I don't want to travel all the way over there, just for her to say no – I shake that thought away, I'm sure she'll say yes!

"Oh by the way," I say to Carlos. "Tell Rob that Gladys gave me all her recipes today, and I'll be doing some practice runs next week, so I'll bring him some mince pies around, and he can give me his very honest opinion," I say, purposely adding a little sarcastic humour.

"You're too good to him," Carlos says, 'I'd have kicked him in the butt for saying that to me."

I laugh at Carlos. "Yeah well...I haven't always been the friend I should have been, I know I've hurt him in the past too," I say, knowing full well that's true.

"Friends!" Carlos laughs, "Can't live with them' – "Can't live without them," we both say, and laugh together. "I'll see you, Carlos."

"Bye sunshine, be safe in the rain."

I wave as he closes the door, and head solemnly towards the elevator.

# FIVE

AS I SIT IN THE CAR waiting for Debs to answer her mobile, I think back to the strange day I've had. It does seem a little odd that no one seems to be interested in gathering together this year, but I quickly shrug it off, knowing it's probably just me.

"Hello?" Debs finally answers.

"Hey, it's me," I say.

"Hey, sis – what's up?"

Debs - my loveable, always bubbly big sister.

"Well...I wanted to invite you guys over for Christmas," I say, with crossed fingers.

"Really?" Debs scoffs.

Seriously, why do I get the feeling that Gladys and Debs seem to think this is the last thing in the world that I am capable of doing? Then I remember that it's most likely because I have never cooked a meal for them – I never had the room in my tiny studio to invite people over.

"Yes, really, I can cook Debs!" I say, laughing a little.

"Oh! – hold on, aren't you going to mom's?" she asks – "Is that aunty Coral?" I hear Lily say.

"Yes darling, but mommy is having a grown-up conversation, you can talk to Aunty Coral in a minute," she tells Lily.

"Mom is not doing Christmas this year Debs, I just found out," I say, it still feels weird.

"She's not doing Christmas?" Debs repeats.

"That's what I said," I say lightly.

"Well...what's she doing?" Debs asks, sounding shocked.

"Spain – she and Malcolm are ditching the holiday and going away, just the two of them."

"You are kidding me!" Debs shouts – a bit like Rob did actually.

"No," I sigh, this is the second time I have been shouted at today.

"Oh my God – Scott, you'll never guess what!" She shouts.

I sigh inwardly. I just want an answer so I can go home to Tristan and have a hug because I'm feeling pretty crap at this very moment. "Debs, can you just let me know if you want to come' – "No, you daft cow, don't you remember me telling you last month when we had the cocktail night about Scott's mom?"

I shake my head and then frown – not recalling any conversation about Scott's mom – I do however remember Debs and I killing ourselves laughing, at what I still don't know, and I remember Tristan helping me to bed, and then nursing my hangover the following day.

"No," I reply.

"We're going up to them," she says.

"To Scotland!" I gasp, "But you never go up there, Scott hates it," I argue – thinking how weird this is.

"I know," she sighs, 'I'm not looking forward to it either. We're flying up Christmas Eve, then flying back Christmas Day evening, the less time spent there, the better, she's such a miserable cow! We were both looking forward to dinner again at moms on Boxing Day – That's pissed me right off that has! Mom can't go away Coral, she just can't!" Debs wails.

And so it is that Debs, Scott and Lily will not be excepting my invitation either. *Why oh why did I think this was a good idea?*

"Yeah...I guess it's their choice," I murmur.

"I bet Erin and Ellie aren't too happy either – I'm gonna call them now!"

I squeeze my eyes shut – I shouldn't have told her. "No Debs! – Don't say anything. Mom and dad are telling everybody next Saturday at dinner – you got an invite, right?"

Debs huffs loudly down the phone. "Yeah..." And now she sounds sad.

"You can come to our place on Boxing Day if you like," I tag on.

Debs sighs. "Maybe..." she says, sounding thoroughly pissed.

I frown again, trying my best not to let all of this affect me. "I gotta go, Debs," I say, and now I sound sad too.

"Yeah...see you later," she says and hangs up.

And trying my best to keep myself up, I remember that I've still got George and Phil to invite, as well as Danny, Joe and her kids. I look out the windscreen at the dark, gloomy clouds that have gathered above me, wondering if it's an omen. Shaking my head at myself, I start the beast up and head home to Tristan.

I AM SAT IN our driveway. I have parked the beast and switched off the engine. However, I have not moved an inch. I feel completely bemused by the events of my day. I just don't understand why everyone is bailing on me – Maybe they secretly don't want to spend it with me? A loud tapping on the window makes me jump a mile, and also makes me realise I must have been out here for a while because it's gone dark outside. I look out the window and find Tristan is stood there, in the pouring rain, looking very concerned.

"Coral?" he shouts, 'what are you doing?"

I quickly come to my senses. And not wanting Tristan to catch a cold from getting soaked, I grab my bag, open the door, take Tristan's hand that's held out, and we both head back inside.

"Babe?" he says as he locks the front door, 'why were you sat out there in the car?"

I turn and look at him. His hair is soaked, beads of water are dripping from his face, and the t-shirt that he's changed into is soaked and completely stuck to him, showing how sexy and defined his body is. My sombre mood is instantly overtaken by desire for this sexy man standing before me – my husband.

"Where's Edith?" I ask breathlessly, as I drop my bag to the floor, then unbutton my coat and throw it on the floor too.

"Actually she's out for a few hours, Christmas shopping," he tells me. *Yes!*

"And Danny?" I pant, as I pull my boots off, throwing them behind me as I do.

Tristan seems very bemused by my odd behaviour. "Staying at Joe's. Coral what the' – I launch myself at him.

As I crash into him, Tristan catches me in his arms, and I kiss him, long and hard. My tongue lapping against his, my legs wrapped around him, my pelvic muscles already contracting as I think about him being inside me.

I pull back gasping. "I want you," I pant.

"Feelings mutual," he says as he turns around and slams me up against the door, and continues to kiss me with so much passion, it moves me. I moan aloud as he presses himself hard against me, I can feel his erection digging into me, the hard sinew of muscle in his legs, his defined arms holding me up, and his ripped abs and chest as we dry hump against the door.

"Fuck Coral," he hisses, as he squeezes my ass cheeks.

## A Christmas Wish

I reach down, find the hem of his t-shirt and rip it off him, and he does the same with me, quickly freeing me of my scarf, jumper and bra. My breasts swell as my nipples harden, just aching for his expertise and his touch. He moans again, bends down, takes my right nipple in his mouth, and sucks, while his left-hand caresses the other.

"Ahhh..." I throw my head back against the door as the feeling heads straight down below, my clit is already throbbing, and I can feel myself already coming. "Tristan..." I gasp. I grab his hair and send my fingernails down his back with my other hand.

He moans a low growl as I do this, and knowing it turns him on so much, I do it again. His head comes up, and I use this as my opportunity to unravel myself from him, then I slam him up against the front door and drop to my knees.

"Coral!" he gasps.

I pull down his sweats, feeling so glad he changed out of his jeans, and his erection springs free, hard and heavy and so deliciously tantalising. I wrap my hand around him, feeling his warmth then taking him in my mouth, I begin to suck, and pull, and fuck him, hard. I love tasting him and seeing him come apart at the seams as I do this.

"Jesus!" He hisses. I look up and see his head is craned back, his muscles bulging, his hands balled into fists as he tries to control himself. So I suck even harder, my tongue swirling around, just the way he likes it. "Stop," he suddenly pants, so I do, and look up at him. "Sofa, now," he orders.

He reaches down, pulls me to my feet, and I jump back up into his arms, pinning my legs tightly around him, still kissing passionately, as Tristan marches us down the hallway. We fall down onto the sofa all tangled up in each other, my hand travelling up and down his back. As his hands caress my breasts, my butt, and then he pulls back and looks down at me.

"Off with these," he says, his voice low and sexy. And within seconds I am stripped of my jeans, pants and socks.

I moan aloud again, I am desperate to feel him inside me. "Tristan," I pant, "In me now," I garble.

He stops, his lips midway up my calf, and smiles so sexily at me, I actually come a little. Then he slowly pushes my legs apart, my muscles ache and protest from our shenanigans this morning, and then he is there – his mouth on me, his tongue lapping and swirling against my already throbbing clit.

"Argh..." I throw my head back, panting with want and

need, and then with his tongue still working its magic on my clit, he pushes a couple of fingers inside me, constantly rubbing against that deliciously sweet spot inside me that he always manages to find. "Ahh..." I moan again, the double sensation of his mouth on my clit, his fingers inside me, pushing and pulling and bringing me right to the edge.

"Christ Coral, you're so fucking wet and ready for me baby," he growls against my clit.

And I come, hard, squeezing against his fingers. "Fuck!" I cry out.

"Oh Coral, you're so fucking sexy!" he gasps, still fucking my clit with his tongue.

And as I open my eyes, my head still buzzing, my body still pulsing wildly as my orgasm rips through me, he leans up, takes his erection in his hand and slowly pushes himself inside me, right to the hilt.

"Tristan!" I mewl aloud at the sensation.

Leaning down and grabbing me by the waist, he pulls me up in one swift movement, so I'm straddling him. "Fuck me," he demands, his eyes dark and sensual.

It's so fucking sexy. *He's so fucking sexy!*

And so I do fuck him. Riding him hard as he pushes himself up into me, and we're building up speed, gyrating against each other like we haven't done this in days. And desperately need the release – and my soul swells and stirs within me as I continue, feeling every inch of him within me, the only sound is our breath coming in sharp gusts, our bodies getting sweatier by the minute.

And I feel it build, sweet, delicious waves hitting me one after the other, rising to a crest that I want so badly to reach with him. And just as I'm about to explode, he looks up at me, his eyes wide and dark, and puts his hand against my face to steady me, then kisses me so slowly and sexily, that I just melt into him – This husband of mine that I love.

With one more deep thrust into me, I come apart at the seams, just as Tristan pounds into me, and then he cries out as he reaches his high too. I watch as he squeezes his eyes shut, sweat pouring from his brow, as he pours himself into me, and then we collapse onto the sofa, entwined in each other's arms. Tristan is on top of me, his head on my chest, my legs wrapped around his as I rhythmically run my fingers through his hair, and we quietly bask in our afterglow.

## A Christmas Wish

I DON'T KNOW how long we actually lie there for, but our breathing has returned to normal, and I suddenly realise why we got so hot and sweaty – The fire is blazing brightly. Tristan must have put it on ready for my return, as it wasn't on when I left earlier today.

His head comes up, pulling me from my thoughts. "Hi," he says, with a chuckle.

"Hi," I chuckle back, and stroke his very handsome face. "Missed you," I whisper because it's the truth and I have.

"Missed you too sweetness," he says and kisses me softly on the lips. "I was starting to worry," he adds, which makes me want to roll my eyes but I don't.

I stare back at him, feeling totally loved up. "Why didn't you call me?" I softly ask.

"I was about to, and then I saw your car outside and realised you weren't in the house," he says, serious now.

"Oh..." I say and smile at my baby.

"What were you doing still sat in the car Coral?" he asks. And I can tell he's trying to keep it light, but there really is an undertone of worry.

I sigh, thinking about today's events. It wasn't all bad, but not all good either. And then I remember Justin, and really not wanting to go into that right now, I decide on a diversion.

"Have you eaten?" I ask – actually feeling hungry after that workout.

"No. You?" he asks.

"No," I reply.

"Not since this morning?" he asks, his brows pulled together in concern.

"No," I sigh.

"You haven't had lunch?" He scolds. *Why oh why didn't I just say yes?*

"No!" I bite.

"Coral' – "What Tristan! Why do you have to keep going on at me about it? I'm hungry now, and I want to eat," I tell him firmly, wondering if now is as good a time as any to have that chat with him.

He sighs and rests his forehead on my chest. "You're killing me," he whispers.

"No!" I reply, '*you're* killing yourself with this. I am happy and healthy Tristan," I softly say, hoping we're not about to get into an argument. He lifts his head, and I can see it in his eyes that is exactly what's about to happen, so I take the bull by the horns.

"Tristan Freeman, if you are about to start arguing with me, after the shitty day I've had, then you can damn well eat on your own, and I'll go down to the Marina, pick Bob up and take him out for tea. At least that way, I won't have anyone nagging me!" *Ugh!*

I try to unpeel him from my body, but he's not to be moved.

"I'm sorry," he whispers, his forehead back on my chest as he softly kisses my sternum.

I sigh, feeling guilty. "Me too," I whisper back. "But I really am hungry Tristan," I add.

His head comes up, his eyes a soft milk chocolate colour. "I'm glad you've said that," he tells me, 'as I have something special planned for you darling." And with that, he slowly pulls himself out of me, which makes us both wince slightly.

"Sore?" I ask, tittering to myself.

"Yes, you sex craved lunatic!" he teases.

I gasp in mock horror. "Don't you like your wife pouncing on you when she gets home?" I tease and wriggle my hips underneath him.

"Of course I do," he says as he gets to his feet, 'but maybe we should take it easy, and hold back for a couple of days?" he adds, looking down at his dick, which admittedly looks a little roar.

"Like that's going to happen," I reply dryly.

Tristan grins widely at me, his dimples on full wattage, and walks towards the downstairs bathroom to clean himself up. As I hear the door close, I turn onto my side and allow the fire to warm my body that seems to be rapidly cooling – probably because I need food. Then I think about what he just said, and my face falls, all humour is gone. *He won't need to worry about us holding back and not having any sex because he won't be here!*

I frown at that thought. I know I shouldn't be feeling so weird about him going away, as he's done before, but I am. I try to shake it off, thinking it's probably just because it's so close to Christmas, and the fact that Edith won't be here either – "Penny for your thoughts?" Tristan asks as he pulls his sweats on commando style.

I throw a fake smile at him. "Nothing," I whisper, and get to my feet. "I'm going to get dressed," I tell him, and start walking towards the stairs so I can clean myself up from our sexing, touch up my makeup, and get into some warm pyjamas.

I hear Tristan following me, and as he reaches me, he entwines his forefinger around my little finger, and we walk up the stairs that way, I know he knows something's up. And I'm reminded again that I haven't felt weird or self-conscious about the fact that I'm fully naked in front of him since we married. Tristan has given me the gift of self-love for my body, and I love him so much for it.

As soon as we are in the bedroom, he sits on the edge of the bed, his elbows on his knees and looks up at me. I consider heading straight into the en-suite to avoid the argument, but his voice stops me.

"What's going on Coral?" he asks – *The interrogation begins!*

I sigh, knowing he's worried, I can see it in his face, and I don't want him to feel like that, so I walk over, and stand in front of him. I run my fingers through his hair as he looks up at me, his puppy dog eyes wide, and I decide on the truth. "I'm feeling weird about you going away," I whisper.

"Oh baby," he soothes, and wraps his arms around my waist, and rests his head against my stomach, and I realise how silly I'm being. I reach down and kiss the top of his head. "Come with me," he says, his tone almost begging.

"I can't now," I tell him.

"Why?" he asks.

"Long story – I'm taking Bob to see Dr Andrews on Monday. He fell over in his studio, and he's not been well. I want a second opinion, and I want and *need* to make sure he's ok, for my own peace of mind," I softly say.

He squeezes me tighter. "Well, why don't you ask Gladys to do it for you?" he suggests.

I shake my head. "No, I want to be there Tristan, and anyway, I'll be fine…I'm just being silly," I whisper, not really sure if I believe my own words.

"I'll cancel," he tells me as he looks up, his big brown eyes pinning me to the floor.

"No. You've been working on this deal for months. You are going. And anyway, if I really do start to feel…weird, I can go and stay at mom's," I say, trying to assure him.

He sighs, still looking up at me.

"I'm fine," I say, purposely rolling my eyes at him with a smile. "Now, would you like to hear about my day? I ask.

"Yes, I would," he says and plants a kiss on my belly.

"Well, can I tell you over dinner – I'm starving," I say, really feeling hungry now.

"I'm not surprised Coral. Granola, blueberries and yoghurt are not going to keep you going all day," he tells me, but in a soft tone so I know he's not going to be argumentative about it. "Come on my darling let me feed you my special treat," he says, as he gets to his feet.

"I need to get cleaned up first," I reply and with a quick kiss on his lips, I head into the en-suite.

AS I STAND in front of the mirror, making the final touches to my makeup, I hear Tristan rummaging around in the bedroom. I frown at my reflection, wondering what he's up to, and then sigh heavily. *What a strange day!* I try to shake it off and manage to do that as I think about the sexy moment we just shared when I got home. Then adding a little lip gloss, I pop my lips, then dab them with a tissue - *You are ready!*

Nodding once to my reflection, I run my fingers rapidly through my hair, so it looks a little wild and sexy, and head out the bathroom. The moment I open the en-suite door, I see a note in Tristan's handwriting sitting on the edge of the bed. I smile widely, walk my naked butt over to it, and pick it up.

*You are an incredibly bright, beautiful woman, who I dearly love.*

*I want to share tonight with you, and show you how much I adore you.*

*Come down when you are ready baby.*

*Tristan*

*xxx*

Tears bubble to the surface at his words. I run over to my bedside cabinet and place his note in my top drawer, with all the other sweet notes and messages I have received from him since we met. I will always keep them. Then, not wanting to be apart from him for a minute longer, I dash into my walk-in closet and dress quickly in my pyjama bottoms, and a vest. Then noticing Tristan's jumper that he hardly ever wears is lying across the chair in the bedroom, I dash over to it, pick it up, inhale his gorgeous scent, and quickly pull it over my head and go in search of Tristan.

# SIX

I RUN DOWN THE stairs in a hurry, and as I do, I realise I can hear a man singing, and he has a wonderful gruff voice, it sounds very melodic and relaxing – but I have no idea who it is. Secondly, I can smell spicy food, and I'd take a wild guess that it's fajitas. I inhale deeply as I run down the stairs, my appetite appreciating the aroma, and as I turn the corner to skip into the living room, I come to an immediate stop when I see him, and what he's done. Tristan is sat on the sofa, in his sexiest dark blue jeans, and a black t-shirt that fits him perfectly. His hands are held together in front of him, his eyes soft and crinkling slightly at the corners as he gazes back at me with a soft, sexy smile, and then everything else starts to register.

Several candles are burning brightly in the room and coupled with the fire, they are creating a beautiful, romantic atmosphere. Our large coffee table has a white cloth over it, and there are lots of plates and bowls that are artfully arranged and filled with brightly coloured food, making my stomach grumble in appreciation. As I take a step closer, I notice two large cushions on the floor in front of the coffee table, two cold bottles of beer, and a bottle of tequila with shot glasses and lime sitting next to it.

I gape at him, in total awe and adoration.

"Baby," he says, as he stands and holds his hand out to me.

I immediately feel underdressed. "I should go change," I manage to whisper.

He smiles sweetly, his dimples on full wattage, and walks towards me. "I don't care what you're wearing," he says. As he reaches me, he wraps his arms around my waist, and then he leans down and kisses me softly, and so sweetly, I am moved again by the moment.

"I don't deserve this," I whisper, looking again at what he's done, and thinking back to me snapping at him about eating lunch – I close my eyes, feeling guilty for that.

"Yes,' he says, softly kissing my lips. My eyes spring open. "You,' another kiss, 'do." And with that, he takes my hand and leads me over to the coffee table. "Take a seat," he says, smiling softly still. I look down at the table in shock. I was not expecting this at all – *Wow!*

As I sink down onto the cushion and cross my legs, I take in the gorgeous display in front of me. There are quesadillas, although I'm not sure what's in them. And chicken, peppers and onions all stir-fried together and sitting in a warming bowl, with a strong fajita scent oozing from them. There are small tortilla wraps, a salad platter of lettuce, cucumber, tomatoes and black olives, guacamole, sour cream, salsa, grated cheese, a black bean dip, and also my favourite, a spicy cheese dip, all steaming hot and ready to dig into. Just looking at it is making my mouth water.

I look up at Tristan in complete awe. "Thank you, baby," I manage to squeak out. "This looks amazing!"

He smiles triumphantly as he sits next to me and crosses his legs too. "A shot?" he asks.

I nod my head like an idiot, unable to actually reply. Tristan picks up the bottle of tequila, two quarts of lime, the salt shaker, and steadily, he fills up the shot glasses.

"I want to try something," he says, 'are you game?" he adds.

I nod again, smiling widely, but wondering what the hell he's about to do.

Picking up a quart of lime, he holds it out to me. "Place the tip between your teeth," he says, 'like this." And I watch how he holds it between his teeth, so it's mostly sticking out of his mouth, and nod.

He leans forward and gently places it on my bottom lip, I bite down to hold it in place, and get a burst of lime on my tongue – *Mmm delicious.*

Then gently taking my hand in his, he holds it palm up, leans down and licks the inside of my wrist, sending tingles in every direction. Then he adds a little salt to the wet spot, licks it off again, takes his shot, and leans forward with the most devilish smile on his face as he sucks the lime that's caught between my teeth, and swallows that too.

That was so hot, and sexy, and - "Fun?" he says, interrupting my thought, as he takes the lime from between my teeth.

"Hell yes!" I giggle, still in awe of my sexy, sweet husband that has evidently gone to a lot of effort to organise all of this.

"Your turn," he says, his sexy grin spreading across his face. *Holy crap!*

Picking up a piece of lime, Tristan places it between his teeth, just waiting for me, challenging me. I pick up the salt, take his hand and lick his wrist, then add the salt and slowly lick it off, keeping my eyes on his the whole time. The salt burns my mouth, so I quickly pick up the shot, neck it back and swallow. The sensation burning and warming me as it flows down to my stomach, then I slowly lean forward, and as seductively as I can, I place my lips around the lime and slowly suck it until I reach the end.

I stay there, close to Tristan's face as I swallow the lime juice and smile widely at him. He takes the lime skin from between his teeth, and grinning widely at me, he leans in a couple of inches and kisses me.

I melt against him, savouring his taste and his skill as his tongue elicits just the right amount of pressure for it to be fun, without getting carried away. Slow seduction is something that my husband is very good at, and I have to say I am one happy customer.

He pulls back swiftly. "Hungry, or do you want to do that again?" he asks with his one eyebrow raised. He knows exactly the effect he has on me, I smile shyly at him.

"Hungry," I whisper. "But we should definitely do that again," I add, feeling a little breathless, and excited.

Tristan smiles widely, wraps his arm around my neck, pulls me towards him and plant a kiss on my temple. "Life will never be boring with you Coral, that is an absolute certainty," he says.

I chuckle aloud at that. "You got that right," I reply dryly, making Tristan laugh too.

"Let's dig in," he says and leans forward to start.

"Wait!" I say, placing my hand on his cheek, and turning him towards me, so we are face to face. "Thank you, Tristan, I really do mean it, all this,' I say, gesturing to the display before us, 'Is a very sweet thing to have done, and I love you very much for it." I lean forward and gently peck his cheek, which has flushed red, but he's smiling shyly, his dimples deep. He nods once, and still smiling, he starts piling chicken onto his tortilla wrap. *He must be hungry!*

We eat in silence for a while, both enjoying the food, but I'm feeling nervous about Justin. I know I shouldn't be, as nothing happened, but it's something I need to share. Otherwise, it will plague me and become a bigger deal than it actually is. So I take a deep breath, ready to begin, then totally chicken out.

"Who's this?" I ask as I pick up a quesadilla and take a bite, my mouth instantly bursting with the taste of three bean chilli and melted cheese, but it's hot, spicy hot, so I quickly dip into the sour cream and take another bite – *So delicious!*

"Singing?" Tristan asks.

I nod as I'm munching again.

"Jack Savoretti – *Before The Storm* album," he tells me. I cock an eyebrow up. "Never heard of him?" He asks, smiling now.

"No, but he's good," I say, which he is, quite folksy, and Tristan must really like him too. I pick up my beer, noticing as I do that its Corona – *He's even got Mexican beer!*

"Cheers," I say, my bottle held out.

Tristan smirks, picks his up and clinks it against mine. "Cheers!" He takes a long draught then turns to me. "So tell me all about your day baby," he lightly adds.

I look down at the food, debating again whether or not to tell him about Justin.

"Coral?" he prompts.

I frown up at him, and deciding now is as good a time as any. I take a deep breath, feeling slightly nervous about his reaction. "I saw Justin today," I say, and take another gulp of beer.

"At your studio?" he says as though it's no big deal.

My head whips back around to him, my eyes almost popping out. "You knew?" I squeak.

He frowns back at me. "Yes. The agency called me a month ago, explained the applicant's situation, and asked if we could come to an agreement for a long-term rental over the winter months. When the deal was done, and a copy of the agreement was emailed to me, I recognised the applicant's name," he tells me.

And I suddenly feel angry at him for not telling me. "Why didn't you tell me?" I ask, trying to keep my cool.

"Because I didn't think it was important," he says, then stops drinking and stares down at me, his eyes dark and foreboding. "Why? Did he do something, or say anything that upset you?" he asks his tone firm.

I frown up at him. "No," I whisper, 'but I still don't understand why you didn't tell me," I add, and take another gulp of

# A Christmas Wish

beer, realising I've nearly finished the bottle. Yet still feeling a little angry that he didn't tell me he knew.

Tristan gets to his feet, heads into the kitchen, and quickly returns with two more bottles of beer. Placing them down in front of us, he sits back down and seems to be contemplating again. Finally, he speaks.

"When the email came through, and I saw his name, at first I was livid that he knowingly had done this, so I made arrangements through the agency to meet with him. And when I did, my gut reaction was to call the whole thing off, but he told me he had no idea it was your studio when he saw the advertisement, and that he really needed this deal. So I thought why not, I have nothing to fear about him being there, do I?" he questions.

I shake my head. "No, you don't," I tell him firmly.

"Good," he breathes, he seems relieved.

And then it hits me. That's why he wanted to come with me today. And why he looked annoyed when I said I was going to see Bob.

"Is that why you wanted to come with me today? Because you knew that Justin was there, or may have been there?" I ask.

He smiles his crooked smile. "Yes, and I'm sorry I didn't tell you. In hindsight, I should have at the time, but I didn't want anything to upset you. The last two months without any drama have been wonderful. I was just trying to protect you," he softly says and reaches up to softly stroke my cheek with his knuckle.

I decide to let it go, the fact that he didn't tell me, but he still needs to know what happened. I take another drink of beer. "Ok, but you should know I bumped into him today," I whisper.

Tristan freezes. "The deal was he keeps away from you," he tells me, 'so if you're telling me that he's harassing you, I'll have him out, tomorrow!" he growls. He does not look happy.

"Tristan," I whisper, and place my hand in his. "It was fine, really," I add.

He stares down at me, searching my face for any hidden truths. "So what happened?" he asks.

I tell him in more detail about Bob falling over and the fact that Justin helped him out. "So, as I left I decided to say thank you to whoever it was," I say, and take another gulp of beer – I'm starting to feel a little woozy.

"That's understandable," Tristan says, 'and that's why you're taking Bob to the doctors?" he adds.

63

I nod once. "Yeah...I'm worried about him Tristan," I frown at the bottle of beer in my hand.

"Hey," Tristan wraps his arm around my waist. "I'm sure he's going to be fine," he softly tells me and kisses my temple.

I blow out a deep breath. "I hope so," I whisper, and try to pull myself out of any sad thoughts about Bob. "Anyway, Justin turned up just as I was walking away, and he invited me in."

I feel him tense beside me, and look up at him. "He invited you in?" He says his voice low. I sigh inwardly, maybe I shouldn't have said anything, but then I change my mind, and decide on the whole truth, that way I have nothing to worry about.

"Yes. It was pouring out, I was getting soaked, he asked me in, so I did and I thanked him for taking care of Bob,' I take a breath and continue. "He offered me a cup of tea, I said no, and then he told me that he missed me and that he still loves me, I told him that's tough, and he should let me go because I am in love with you and I would never, ever leave you. Then we chatted about what we were both doing for Christmas and he offered to call if something happens to Bob, so I gave him our landline. We wished each other a Merry Christmas, and I left." I take two gulps of beer, feeling glad I managed to get it all out.

Tristan is gazing at me with warm eyes, as though he's totally in love.

"What?" I ask, feeling all shy again.

"You were nervous about telling me," he says.

I nod once and take another gulp of beer, noticing I'm almost two bottles down.

"You shouldn't have been," he softly says, then leans forward and gently places his lips on mine. "I trust you, implicitly," he whispers against my lips, his big chocolate eyes melting me again.

I smile back at him, feeling so much better for it. "I trust you too," I whisper back.

Tristan chuckles then and seems to relax again. "So what else happened?" he asks. And my worry about Justin is forgotten, so I launch into the story about the rest of my day.

"So we only have Bob coming over?" Tristan says.

"Yes," I sigh, trying not to feel sad about it all again.

Tristan gazes back at me. "I know you're sad about it, but honestly, I'm relieved," he says, totally surprising me.

"You are?" I squeak.

He nods once. "Coral, I don't want you hosting at all. It's a lot of work, and I know how stubborn you are. You wouldn't have allowed me to help you, so I'd have had no choice but to stand back, watching you get stressed, which you would have done, and I don't want that for you." He tells me firmly.

I gape at him. "I wouldn't have got stressed," I argue.

He cocks an eyebrow up at me.

"Ok, maybe a little stressed," I chuckle.

"Exactly!" he says, 'and you've been through enough, we both have. And I think we deserve a happy, relaxed Christmas," he says.

"You mean a sexy one!" I retort dryly.

He smiles his crooked smile again and chuckles slightly. "Well I'm not going to say no to that," he says, making me giggle.

AFTER ANOTHER HOUR of eating Tristan's delicious spread, drinking more tequila shots and beer, and talking and laughing the whole time, I feel well and truly relaxed, and I have to say, a little drunk. As I stagger slightly towards the downstairs bathroom, I have to wonder if Tristan planned to get me drunk - *Hmm...tequilla!*

I wobble slightly as I stand to wash my hands, and try to focus on my blurry reflection. Then as I'm attempting to dry my hands, I hear Edith come home, chat for a moment with Tristan, then head up the stairs. I frown slightly, knowing that if Tristan and I end up having sex again, we're going to have to be quiet, and I hate having to do that.

A light bulb moment strikes! I decide that when I finally get around to talking to Tristan about moving, that we should buy a place that has a separate annexe for Edith and Danny, that way, we don't have to worry about anyone walking in on us. I nod several times at my reflection and congratulate myself on such a fantastic idea. I then start to smile, widely, for absolutely no reason at all – *Must be the tequila!*

With that thought in mind, I turn towards the door and attempt to unlock it. I realise of course that the door, not opening has nothing to do with the door, but my incapacity to unlock it, which makes me burst into a fit of giggles. I try several times, still laughing uncontrollably, to unlock the bathroom door, until I finally get it right. *Phew!*

Standing up tall, and trying to hide the fact that I feel tipsy, I look down the hallway and see Tristan sitting on the sofa, noticing he looks very happy and serene.

*Hmm...My sexy man!*

I manage to take a few steps without wobbling and thinking I'm doing so bloody fantastically, I stop concentrating on the task of reaching the sofa, and end up falling over my own two feet, which I think is fucking hilarious!

*Why is everything so funny when you're drunk?*

Tristan is stood above me, shaking his head, but he's smiling. "You ok?" he chuckles.

"Yes!" I manage to say between fits of giggles, 'I fell over,' I add.

"I know," Tristan says as he bends down to me. "You're so cute when you're drunk baby," he says and helps me to my feet. Then he leads me over to the sofa and gently sits me down. "I think we should go to bed," he softly says.

*Mmm...bed with my sexy man* – I lean forward to kiss him and almost topple over, but Tristan catches me in time – I'm giggling again.

"I don't mean for that," he tells me.

"Then I want to stay here and watch Scrooge," I manage to slur. It happens to be my favourite Christmas film because it's funny and it has Bill Murray in it, and I want Tristan to see it. There are so many films he hasn't seen because of working all the time. "You work too hard," I add.

Tristan smiles widely at me. "We can watch it in bed," he replies, and I notice his tone is firm. *He's telling me off!*

"Tristan!" His lips reach mine, silencing whatever it is I was about to say, and now he's done that, I can't remember what it is I *was* about to say. "Bed!" He says, and before I can argue, he's lifted me up into his arms, and he's carrying me up the stairs.

Reaching our room, he places me on the bed, undresses me and starts the movie. "Get under the covers darling, I'll be back in a minute," he says, and so I do.

There are two Bill Murray's – I squeeze one eye shut as I try to focus on him, but it doesn't help. I sit up and try to focus on the film, the words, but decide I could be here all night and flop back down onto the pillows.

Finally, Tristan is back in the room. "Where have you been?" I ask, very sleepily now.

"Switching everything off, and getting you some water," he says, I kind of notice he has something in his hand. "Here baby, take these," he says.

I struggle to sit up, but take the tablets from him, dropping them twice onto the bed, so Tristan takes over. He manages to get them on my tongue and then keeping hold of the glass of water he gently tips it up so I can get a good couple of gulps to swallow the tablets.

"Ok?" he asks, chuckling now.

I nod my head as I can hear his words, but somewhere at the back of my mind, I don't understand how I got this drunk. I flop back down onto my pillow and hug it tightly.

"Sleep now baby," he whispers and kisses my cheek.

"'Kay," Is the last thing I remember saying...

# SEVEN

THE FOLLOWING morning I wake to the sound of the wind howling, and the rain lashing against the window. I guess we're having another storm, which makes me feel crappy because we have to go Christmas shopping today, and that means facing the weather. *Ugh!* Just the thought of the cold wind and the icy rain makes me pull the duvet up over my head, wanting nothing more than to stay in bed all day. Why can't we get snow like other countries? It's much prettier and much nicer than wind and rain!

With that thought in mind, I turn on my side and reach out for Tristan, only to find he's not there, and I hate it when that happens. Slowly sitting up, I look outside and see it most definitely is another storm. I can see huge grey clouds, and it's so dark and miserable, that it feels like night time. I immediately have a panicky moment with that thought – *Have I slept through the whole day?* - I look up at the clock on the wall – 8.35am. *Phew!*

I instantly feel relieved, and as I scan my surroundings, I notice my clothes from last night are neatly folded on the chair in the corner, and then I notice a big glass of veggie juice sat on my bedside table – *Yummy!*

Leaning forward, and only just recognising that I don't seem to have a hangover, I pick up the glass. It's cold, so I'm guessing Edith or Tristan has recently been up here. Feeling very dehydrated, I don't stop drinking until I have finished it all. And then with a defeated sigh, I look out the window and decide that there's is nothing I can do about the fact that I suggested going shopping, and I don't really want to go back on it, so placing my glass down, I slide out of bed.

As I do, I have another weird moment about Tristan going away. I immediately brush it off, then I stomp into the bathroom, quickly wash my face, clean my teeth, and then I throw my winter robe on, so I can go in search of him. Taking the stairs two at a time, I come to a stop as I enter the living area, as Tristan is sat at the breakfast bar, eating – *He's always eating!*

"Good morning," he says, smiling widely at me.

"Hi," I croak, feeling happy to see him and head over to the breakfast bar.

"Breakfast?" Tristan asks as I sit next to him.

I shake my head. "No thanks, just coffee," I quietly say. Ok, maybe I am a little hung over. I feel a bit woozy from running down the stairs.

"How are you feeling?" Tristan asks as he pours coffee into my mug then adds some cream. *He's using his mind reading skills again!*

"Ok," I say, trying to sound perky. "Eat up, we're in a hurry," I tell him.

"We are?" he says.

My face falls, he hasn't remembered. "Um…yeah, Christmas shopping?" I croak and take a sip of coffee.

"Coral look," Tristan says, nodding towards the hallway. I turn and see four huge brown boxes, and three tall white boxes sat in the hallway.

"What's that?" I whisper.

"Christmas decorations," Tristan says.

My head whips back round to him, my mouth gaping open. "Christmas Decorations?" I whisper back.

His face falls. "Have I got it wrong?" he asks. I frown at him, not understanding what he means. He turns to face me and takes my hand in his. "Yesterday, when I asked Edith to help me organise dinner for us, we were chatting about the decorating, and she suggested ordering online as it's what her daughter does every year," he says, 'what do you think?" he asks.

I gaze back at him, as I'm not really sure how I *do* feel about it. One the one hand, it's bloody fantastic that he's done this, I don't think I'd have done that well with crowds of people today, or the frigging storm. But on the other hand, I thought it would be really magical for us to do this together, I imagined us picking out items we liked, ones we thought would look good in our house, I thought it would be a really fun day out.

"Coral?" Tristan prompts, but I don't answer him as I'm kind of speechless, and have brain fog from too much alcohol last night.

"Coral?" he prompts again, 'talk to me, darling."

My mouth opens and closes once, and then I think of the other reason we were meant to be shopping. "What about Edith's present?" I squeak, panicking now as she's going away tomorrow.

"Sorted," Tristan says, and my anxiety about it is immediately quashed.

My mouth pops open again, as I gawp at him. I blink several times, trying to get my brain to fire. "Ok,' I whisper, 'what did you get?" I add, frowning now.

"A new necklace with a cross, some perfume, and a first edition collection of the Brontë sisters," he casually says, as though he's just bought her soap. This time my chin hits the floor. Tristan smiles warmly at me, leans forward, and softly brings my chin up, so my lips meet again.

'Coral' – "First edition?" I squeak, it's the first thing I can think of to say.

Tristan's serious now. "Yes, she's a huge Brontë fan."

I blink several times again, trying to think of the next thing to say or ask. "How much was that?" I whisper, staring back at him with wide eyes.

"Are you concerned about the amount I have spent' – "No!" I balk, realising what he's just about to ask. "No Tristan...that's the sweetest..." I stop as he's looking at me with big round, puppy dog eyes that are just melting me. So without another word, I step up onto his stool and sit on his lap, which he helps me to do, then wrap my arms around his neck.

"Tristan Freeman, you are the most thoughtful...sweetest man I have ever known," I softly tell him then plant my lips on his for a chaste kiss. "But I am intrigued," I whisper.

"How much first editions are?" He asks, reading my mind again.

I nod back at him.

"They were almost three grand," he tells me.

My eyes widen. "Wow!" I gasp.

"I think she'll like them," he says, sounding very proud of himself.

I shake my head in wonder. "Tristan, I...I would have got her such a terrible present compared to that," I chuckle, 'I didn't think you knew her that well," I add.

He nods once and squeezes me around the waist.

"And the cross?" I ask.

"Haven't you noticed Edith is always out Sunday mornings?" He asks.

A Christmas Wish

I frown and then think about it. I suppose she is, but I've never really thought about why. "What's that got to do with a cross?" I ask.

Tristan smiles animatedly at me. "She's a Christian who goes to church every Wednesday and Sunday," he tells me.

"Oh..." I whisper, the penny finally dropping – That explains the cross. "So why have you got her the necklace?" I ask, presuming she already has one. In fact, I think I have seen her wearing one.

"She always wears one, but she gave hers to Danny, so I wanted to get her another as a gift," he tells me. My mouth gapes open *again*.

"She gave it to Danny?" I squeak. I know things like that are very important to religious people.

Tristan chuckles at me, leans in and kisses my cheek. "You are so sweet and funny baby," he leans in again, and nuzzles my neck, then plants his lips there, on my skin, which send sparks of desire straight down below.

"Tristan," I whisper, and lean my head back so he can have better access to my neck, but my brain rejects the movement. My head starts throbbing big slow thuds, so I know it's only going to get worse as the day goes on. "Ow," I lean forward and hold my head in my hands.

"Headache?" Tristan softly asks, holding my hands in his.

"Yeah," I croak, feeling sorry for myself.

"Here baby." I open my eyes and watch as Tristan leans forward and picks up the tablets he's already placed on the breakfast bar, along with my coffee, then hands the cup and the tablets to me.

"Thanks," I croak again and swallow the painkillers.

Tristan smiles sympathetically at me. "Eating will help," he softly says, and I know he's right. But I do not want to get into another fight about food.

"I know," I whisper, 'just let me wake up first," I add, which makes him chuckle, and then I remember my original question. "So why did Edith give her cross to Danny?" I ask.

Tristan's serious now. "I guess it's to help him," he says, then frowns at those words. "I think it's because she knows he's been through so much, and she wanted to help guide him maybe," he ponders that thought. "Some Christians believe that wearing the cross offers protection from evil, in whatever form that may come in, so maybe it's about that," he says, and I know he's not really sure.

I shake my head in amazement. "That must have been such a big deal for her to do that," I whisper.

Tristan nods. "Yeah, I think it was," he says.

"Have you seen Danny wearing it?" I ask, hoping he is.

"I'm not in the habit of looking at what Danny's wearing," he replies sarcastically, which makes me laugh.

"You know what I mean," I chuckle, and then my stomach rumbles, and we look up at one another. Tristan's face falls, and I know he's about to say something, so I place my forefinger against his lips.

"I'll have boiled eggs with marmite soldiers," I whisper, then crack a huge smile.

His wide grin reflects mine. "Coming right up," he says.

"Wait!" I say, clutching his arms so he can't slide me from his lap. "The decorations," I add, looking down and frowning at myself. I'm still not quite sure how I feel about it.

"You're not happy," Tristan says, his head cocked to the side as he reads me.

"No, it's not that..." I look up at him then shake my head. He looks hurt, and the last thing in the world I want to do is hurt him.

"Be honest with me," he whispers, and leans his forehead against mine, 'we promised that we would be," he adds, and I know he's right.

I sigh heavily. "I want to be, but I don't want to hurt your feelings," I tell him.

Tristan chuckles and takes my face in his hands, so I have no choice but to look up at him. "Tell me," he orders, but his tone is soft and full of love.

I smile softly at him. "Ok...well, I just thought...it would be nice to do it together. I get to know what you like, and vice versa,' I shrug once, then I think we have such similar tastes that he's probably picked the exact items I would have picked. 'I guess I just thought it would be fun, I've never done anything like that before and as it's our first Christmas," I stop talking because Tristan is smiling widely at me. "What?" I whisper.

"I bought every Christmas Decoration they had Coral so we can do exactly that," he says.

I gawp at him again. "Oh..." And for the second time this morning, my chin hits the floor. Tristan is chuckling again as he nuzzles my neck once more. He seems very happy and relaxed today.

## A Christmas Wish

My brain finally fires a question. "Um...what are we going to do about the ones we don't want?" I ask.

His head comes up. "Give them to a charity?" he suggests, but I suddenly have a better idea, which also reminds me that I haven't spoken to Tristan about this yet, he doesn't know.

"I have a better idea," I say, feeling quite proud of myself.

"You do?" he laughs, his head cocked to the side.

"Yes. We could give them to the charity I donate to every year," I tell him.

His face suddenly falls, all humour is gone, as he gazes back at me with wide eyes.

"What?" I whisper, suddenly feeling self-conscious.

"You donate to a charity?" he says, he seems utterly shocked.

I sigh inwardly as I think back to what happened when I was sixteen, and the reason I continue to help with this particular charity. "Yeah...to The Clock Tower Sanctuary here in Brighton, £250 every Christmas," I whisper, frowning now.

Tristan's face softens. "What kind of charity is it baby?" he asks.

I swallow hard and avert eye contact. "A homeless shelter... for young people...actually it's more than that, and the name fits, because it *is* a sanctuary," I say, my voice shaking slightly.

Tristan squeezes me tightly around the waist. "There's more," he whispers and gently lifts my chin, so I have to look at him.

I nod slightly, remembering it all so clearly.

"Will you share it with me?" he asks. I debate for a moment, not really sure if I want him to know this part of me, the aggressive, angry young girl I once was. "Please..." he whispers.

I nod once, decision made, then I take a breath and begin. "Ok, so you know I was...getting myself into trouble in school and that I ended up expelled and homeschooled," I whisper, and he nods, his face dead serious. "Ok, well...what I didn't say was that I..." I squeeze my eyes shut, trying not to get angry about it because what I did was terrible, unforgivable – although I was forgiven, and I didn't deserve it.

"Hey," Tristan whispers, 'don't talk about it if you don't want to baby," he softly says.

I open my eyes, look up at him and start blurting it all out. "You have to understand Tristan. I was so angry...all of the time, I felt like a freak but I had to constantly hide it, and eventually, that takes its toll. It wasn't long before my exams were due, and I had this huge bust-up with Debs. Gladys wasn't there to calm

73

everything down, so I really let go, and so did Debs. We both said such awful things to one another, and she really hit home with a lot of the things she was saying to me, which just made me angrier," I take another breath. "And...I...I just lost it...and I attacked her," I manage to say, tears pricking my eyes as I think back to it all, to how much I hurt Debs and all the drama that unfolded afterwards.

Tristan wraps his arms around my shoulders, and I sink my head onto his shoulder. "Do you hate me for doing that?" I whisper.

"No baby," he softly says, his arms holding me tightly.

I sniff once and continue because he needs to know the whole story. "Luckily, Scott came home. He found us in the living room, pulled me off Debs and threw me out the house. I found out later that I'd actually broken her nose," I say, wincing at the memory.

Tristan hisses at that. "You must have one hell of a right hook," he says. And I know he's trying to lighten the moment, but it doesn't forgive my behaviour that day.

I take a breath, slowly blow it out and continue. "So, I bang on the door several times to try and get back in, because it was pissing down and freezing cold, but Scott wasn't having any of it, which at the time made me even angrier, but looking back, it was the best thing for me." I look up at Tristan. "I hadn't realised what I'd done Tristan, it was like coming out of a trance, and at the time, I just thought I'd thrown a couple of punches like Debs had, but I guess not..." I look down again, feeling ashamed and continue.

"Of course, in my angry state, I debated breaking one of the windows, but I knew Gladys would have gone mad at me for doing that, so I stormed off." I glance out the window, and see the storm is really kicking up now. "I paced the beach for hours, trying to figure out what to do, but I was getting soaked and colder by the minute. I thought about going to Joyce's, but I didn't think she would let me in, because I figured Scott would have called her and told her what I'd done," I take another deep breath. "I basically came to the conclusion that this was it. I was never going back because I figured nobody *would* want me back, and that from now on I was homeless... living on the streets." Tristan tenses beneath me, but stays silent.

I shake my head at myself. "Survival mode kicked in like it did as a kid. I figured I needed dry clothes, so I knew I would need to steal some, and then I thought I'd better find somewhere dry to spend the night. I can remember thinking that it was going to be really hard you know, being so cold, so I thought about stealing a sleeping bag too." I chuckle at that part.

"I can remember being so cold by the time I made the decision to walk into town that my legs wouldn't work properly, and I was shaking violently, but I made it. And call it divine intervention, or chance, but I bumped into this woman. And I mean literally smashed into her as I wasn't looking where I was going, she almost fell over, but I grabbed her hand and stopped the fall. She took one look at me and said 'Honey, you're soaked through, don't you have anywhere to go?' And without thinking about it, I just shook my head at her. She told me she volunteered at a place where I could get into dry, clean clothes and have a hot meal. So I did exactly that, I followed her, she signed me in, got me some dry clothes, and sorted a bowl of stew out for me."

I smile up at Tristan. "It was The Clock Tower Sanctuary. I didn't know at the time, but they specifically help young people who find themselves with no home to go to, so they end up living on the street. The Sanctuary gives them a place to shower, to eat, to wash their clothes, and eventually off the streets and into accommodation. The volunteers are amazing, and they run all kinds of free classes, alcohol and drugs, sex education, emotional counselling..." I drift off for a moment, remembering how adamantly I said no to that.

"They really helped me, Tristan. I stayed that night in emergency accommodation, which was a tiny room with a single bed and that's it, not that I slept. The next day, I went back to the centre as soon as it opened, only to find John and Joyce waiting for me. And at first, I panicked, and I was about to run, but Joyce looked so upset. She started telling me all about how frantic Gladys had been, and that they'd been looking for me all night," I hide my head under Tristan's chin, just waiting for his disgust, his reprimand, anything that would justify him being upset with me.

"Christ Coral," he whispers and squeezes me tight. "I cannot believe you nearly ended up living on the streets," he softly croaks.

I nod my head once. "It was my own fault, Tristan. I attacked Debs. I deserved the punishment."

"The punishment you decided to dish out on yourself!" he scolds, unhappy now.

"I was disgusted with myself," I bite back. "Especially when I found out how much I'd hurt her."

Tristan sighs heavily. "So what happened afterwards?" he asks.

I swallow hard. "Gladys was relieved but really angry with me for running away and what I did to my sister. Debs and Scott moved in with John and Joyce because they didn't want to be in the same house as me, which I can understand, but they did come back six months later."

"Families," Tristan whispers.

"Debs forgave me, eventually. It took a lot of convincing from Gladys, who reminded Debs that she was as much to blame and that it takes two people to cause a fight." I can't help smiling as I think about how Gladys handled it all. "Gladys made us both tell her what we'd actually said to each other. And she pointed out to Debs that although I had said some horrible things, that hers were far worse because she was older, and should have known better and that saying I wasn't wanted, and that she wished I had never been born, and that she thinks I'm a weirdo was enough to push most people over the edge," I sigh heavily. "So that's why The Sanctuary gets my hard earned money every year, because it's very well deserved, and they help young people in trouble, they helped me." I add.

"One hundred thousand," Tristan pipes up, surprising me.

I sit up so I can see him properly. "For them?" I squeak out in disbelief.

He smiles widely at me. "Absolutely," he says, 'I'll get Karen to sort the Bankers Cheque, so when I get back next week, we can take the decorations and the money over to them."

"Tristan," I whisper, totally moved by his offer, and lean my forehead against his, 'thank you, so much," I whisper with closed eyes. I can't help thinking about how much they can do with that amount, and how many young kids they can save.

"They saved you my darling, and now you're my wife and my home," he whispers back. "It's the least I can do."

I open my eyes and look up at him, actually feeling glad that I shared that with him. "Thank you," I croak, trying to hold back the tears.

He smiles widely, leans forward and pecks my lips. "Right then, as we have a full day of decorating to do, I better get on and feed you," he says, gently sliding me off his lap.

"I can make it," I protest. "You cooked last night!"

"What was our deal?" he asks as he lifts me up and plonks me down on my breakfast stool.

"Deal?" I question.

"Yes, what was our deal when it came to being drunk, and dealing with hangovers?" He asks. Oh! Now I know what he means - *Brain is definitely not firing on all cylinders!*

I smile up at him. "That we make sure we look after that drunken person, get them safely to bed, and take care of them the next day," I say.

"Exactly!" he says, and with a chaste kiss on my lips, he heads into the kitchen and begins cooking up my breakfast.

I try to think back to the last time I was drunk, and that was when Debs was here. I ponder that for a second and come to the realisation that I don't use alcohol as an escape anymore, which is amazing, considering how much I would turn to it, without really knowing that's what I was doing, not until I met Tristan.

He was the one that brought it to light. I dread to think how I would have ended up had it not been for him. *A crazy bat-shit old woman, who smells of pee and is always pissed that's how!* I shudder at the very thought of it. And then I remember last night and my thought that Tristan had got me drunk on purpose.

"Did you plan on getting me drunk?" I ask.

"I didn't get you drunk,' he laughs, 'you got yourself drunk." I frown back at him. "Coral, don't you remember? You kept wanting more shots of tequila, and after the fifth, I said no more, that's when you continued with the beer."

"Oh," I whisper, looking down at the breakfast bar.

"I think you wanted more of the tequila because you really liked the game," he says with a wink.

I smile coyly at him, he's right, it really was fun, shame it didn't go anywhere. Then again, we have been at it like rabbits lately, so probably best to take it easy and let our bodies heal. And just as I think that I get a really naughty idea come to mind, so I decide to shock him, just so I can see his reaction.

"Yeah, I did enjoy it," I say, 'but next time, let's lick the salt from a more interesting place, like my nipples," I add.

"Fuck!" He shouts as the egg he's about to add to boiling water slips from his fingers and splatters all over the floor.

And knowing it had the desired effect, I can't help giggling raucously as Tristan turns to me with a look of shock spread across his face. He slowly shakes his head from side to side, but he can't help smiling at me as I manage, somehow, to get down from the stool, walk into the kitchen, and help him clean up the mess.

# EIGHT

I SMILE WIDELY as I stare up at the very large Christmas Tree that's been erected in the living room, right next to the fireplace. As promised, Edith has been cheerfully helping, on the proviso that Tristan put her Kings College Christmas Carols Album on his big stereo, which he did, and turned it up loud so it could be heard throughout the whole house. And right now, O Holy Night is playing, and even though I don't know all the words, I hum along as I reach up and place another bauble on the tree.

Then I turn, chuckling away to myself because Edith is merrily dancing around the kitchen, singing away as she places little Christmas ornaments that we picked out in strategic places around the kitchen, and right now she's changing the oven gloves and hand towels to Christmas ones. And I feel wonderful, and loved, and happy because we are almost done. It's almost dark outside too, so we'll be able to turn the Christmas lights on that are all over the house, which I'm hoping will make it feel like a magical Christmas grotto, all of our own.

I gaze out the window, thinking about how much life has changed again. It really does feel like I'm living in a dream sometimes. My mind wonders to Joyce, and I feel annoyed again that I didn't get to speak to her today, in fact, no-one even answered the phone. I close my eyes for a moment and push the annoyance away because I don't want to feel like that. But at least I remembered to get Bob booked in with Dr Andrews - I'm surprised I didn't forget in my hungover state - which makes me laugh at myself, and I'm back to where I was a moment ago.

Tristan appears, grinning from ear to ear with something in his hand. He walks over to me, and without a word, he bends down and plants a sweet kiss on my lips.

"Hi," he whispers.

"Hi back," I giggle because I can't help it – I'm just so damn happy.

"Look what I have!" He says with the most animated smile on his face as he holds two bags up in the air - I instantly realise they're chocolate Christmas coins, which makes me giggle again.

"Two bags?" I laugh, knowing I won't be eating many of them as I find them too sweet.

His face falls, and I immediately feel guilty.

"I never had these as a kid," he says, 'or as an adult," he adds with a frown, which makes me think of the wicked witch he once dated, Olivia, and how she used him for all those years – *Ugh!*

"Hey," I wrap my arms around his waist and pull him close to me. "I'm sorry baby, I didn't know that," I whisper, feeling even guiltier now he's told me that – *Me and my big mouth!*

His frown slowly subsides. "It's stupid...I know," he says with a sigh.

My face falls. "Tristan," I say, serious now. "You put as many of those babies on the tree as you want to," I softly tell him, squeezing my arms around him. "In fact, how many bags did you get?" I ask.

"Four." His answer is immediate, so now I know this really is a big deal to him.

"Right, well why don't we put two on this tree, one on the tree in the hallway, and one on the tree in our bedroom?" I cheerfully ask. His face lights up as though he *is* a kid, and it *is* Christmas Day, and Father Christmas has most definitely been.

"Good idea baby!" he says, and with another peck on the lips, he gets to work.

Feeling triumphant that I managed to bring him back to a happy place, I walk over to the kitchen, as I do believe its wine time. We all deserve it after working so hard today to make the house look so nice, but as I move around the kitchen, I can't help watching Tristan. And as I do, I get the strangest image come to me of Tristan as a boy decorating a small Christmas Tree in a very small living room. And he's happy and grateful and still enjoying himself – yet I know how much he struggled with being so poor – and then the image is gone.

Frowning at that odd moment, I grab the wine out of the fridge and pop the cork. Reaching up to the cupboard for the glasses, Danny thankfully appears, and hands four glasses to me, and I think for the millionth time that we really should re-arrange where they are - my short arse can't reach up that high.

"Coral, I have something to tell you," Danny whispers, smiling widely – The happiness in this house must be infectious.

"You do?" I say, smiling back as I pour wine into our glasses.

He's suddenly serious, and I can tell he's struggling for the right words to say, as I very often do.

"Are you ok Danny?" I ask, and gently touch his forearm, knowing he still has deep issues with touch, as I once did – and I still do with strangers. *So yeah, I'm still a little bit fucked up!*

He swallows hard and nods once, keeping his eyes down to the floor.

"Whenever you're ready," I softly tell him and pop the remaining wine back in the fridge. Back at Danny's side, I hand him a glass, which he accepts and knocks back a big mouthful. And I recognise the sign, he's nervous, so to try and make him feel more comfortable by giving him some space, I pick up Tristan's glass, as Edith seems to have disappeared, and begin to walk away.

"Wait!" he says, stopping me in my tracks. I watch as he puts his glass down, and reaches into his jeans pocket. "You remember I talked to you the other day about how much I like Joe," he asks.

"Yeah...?" I reply, wondering where this is going.

"Well, I've decided I'm going to ask her to marry me." And I'm not shocked by this news, I've kind of been expecting it with how much Joe has expressed her love for him, but I smile widely at Danny. And out of his jean pocket, he produces a small black velvet pouch then he pulls the string open and tips the contents into his hand. "What do you think? Well, what I mean is, do you think she'll like it?" he asks.

Sat in his hand is a ring - A small, delicate, very pretty square diamond, gold engagement ring.

"Danny," I whisper, and place Tristan's wine back down onto the side. I carefully pick up the ring and inspect it. "It's beautiful," I whisper, knowing it will really suit Joe. She's tiny and delicate and has really slim fingers so it will look gorgeous on her.

"Do you think she'll like it?" he asks again, and I can tell he's nervous.

"Yes Danny, I really do," I say, looking him in the eye, so he knows I mean it, which makes him smile, in fact, I would say he looks relieved. "If you were worried, you could have asked me to come with you and help you choose," I say, smiling at his happy expression.

# A Christmas Wish

His face falls. "I didn't think of that," he says, and now he looks annoyed with himself.

I chuckle at him. "Well, you don't need to think about that now, because I think it's perfect, I think she'll love it," I tell him.

"That's good," he says, 'you won't say anything will you?" he asks, as I hand him the ring back and he safely stows it away in his jean pocket.

"No," I whisper, 'of course not Danny. Have you decided when you're going to ask her?" I add, keeping my voice low.

Danny starts to perspire, he looks really nervous again. He shakes his head and takes another gulp of wine. "I'm bricking it," he finally says.

"Are you worried she'll say no?" I ask.

He shakes his head again. "I kind of asked her the other day if she wanted to get married again, and she said yes, then joked that she's waiting for me to ask her, but I knew it wasn't a joke."

I frown up at him because even though Joe has told him that, he doesn't look so sure. "Sounds to me like she can't wait to marry and settle with you," I tell him.

"I know," he sighs, 'it's just I wanted to make a big deal out of it and ask her on Christmas Day, but to be honest Coral, I don't think I'll make it. I don't think I can contain it for that long," he says. And he looks like he's having a mini panic attack.

I put my hand on his upper arm to try and calm him. "Then get it done Danny. It doesn't have to be a big deal. I mean...as in, it doesn't have to be all bells and whistles, and all the crap you see in films. If I were in your shoes, I would ask her – like tonight. I'd go over, get down on your knee, present her with the ring, and ask. That way, you're not worrying for the next three weeks and ruining your own Christmas with, will she, won't she questions buzzing around in your head."

Danny looks down at me, and again I'd say he looks relieved. "You're right," he says, 'why didn't I think of that – just get it done!"

And taking me by complete surprise, he wraps me up in a bear hug, which I reciprocate. "Thank you Coral,' he whispers in my ear, 'you've changed my life you know, I can't tell you how thankful I am."

"We all love you, Danny," I whisper back, squeezing him tightly, and I feel relieved I said the right thing because ever since Danny came to be with us, which I think was absolutely meant to be, he's felt like a brother to me. He is my family, and I love him just as much as I love Gladys and Debs and now

Malcolm. And that includes Edith too. And because of that, I know I would fiercely love and protect him, for the rest of my life.

He pulls back and smiles down at me. "Do you think Tristan will be ok if" – "Take my car," I whisper, knowing he has the spare key for when he escorts me to work and back.

He blows out a deep breath. "Ok," he says, and takes the last gulp of wine. "Wish me luck," he says.

I can't help smiling broadly at him. "Good luck, and send me a text, so I know the answer. Otherwise, I'll be worried about you," I firmly tell him.

"Will do boss," he says and chuckles once.

"Get out of here!" I say, laughing too. And I watch him walk towards the front door, open it, he nods once to me, and then he's gone – *Whoa!*

"What's wrong Coral?" Tristan asks from behind me. *Damn it!*

"Nothing," I lie, turning to look at him. I hand him his wine and clink my glass against his, then take a well-needed sip.

"Where's Danny gone?" Tristan asks. *Oh, holy bollocks!*

"Oh...he said something about picking a present up from one of the stores," I say, shrugging my shoulders as though I have no idea.

"Ok," Tristan says, smiling widely at me.

"What?" I ask – he's looking at me that way again.

"Come here you," he says, and placing our wines down, he pulls me into him, and wraps his arms around me, squeezing me tight – too tight.

"Can't breathe," I manage to whisper.

Tristan chuckles but releases his superhero grip on me, and I rest my chin on his chest and look up at him. It's strange to think that it was only two months ago, at the beginning of October, when Kane attacked us, so much more time seems to have passed. Yet when I look up at Tristan, I'm reminded that it's only been a few weeks really since he's been completely healed. And like me, he's been left with scars too. One on his hairline from Susannah's attack, and one across his left eyebrow from Kane's attack. His skin was split so badly that they had to put in a few stitches once the swelling had gone down, but with a cold compress on his bruises every day, he soon began to recover.

And the image of him cold and not breathing on the pool room floor floods my mind again – *Argh! Go away!*

# A Christmas Wish

I close my eyes and rest my forehead on his chest for a moment.

"Baby, there's something I wanted to ask you?" He says which takes my mind off the memory replaying.

"Fire away," I whisper, but as I look up at him, I can see this is hard for him to say. His cheeks are flushed, his brow furrowed, and he's clenching his teeth.

Tristan takes a deep breath. "Last year...' he takes another breath and slowly blows it out. 'Last year, I placed a Christmas Wreath on my folks..." he stops again and takes a moment. "On their grave," he finally adds.

I reach my hand up and gently touch his cheek. "You want to do the same this year?" I softly ask.

He nods his head, and I can tell he's fighting back the tears – *Oh Tristan!*

"Of course Tristan, you just say when you want to go," I whisper, feeling my heart break for him.

"Thank you," he croaks and wraps his arms around me again for a moment. Then with a kiss on the top of my head, he says, "Baby, I better go and pack...ready for tomorrow. I've got an early start in the morning, and I don't want to be doing it then."

I look up at him, and with a bright smile but heavy heart, I nod my reply...

THE FOLLOWING MORNING, Tristan wakes me with a kiss on my forehead. I blink my eyes open and see it's pitch black outside, the clock on the wall reads 5.15am. The bedside lamp is on, creating a soft orange glow in the room. I look across at Tristan who's sat on the chair, tying up the laces on his very shiny shoes. He's evidently showered, as he smells fucking fantastic, he's clean shaven, and his hair is artfully combed into place as he always does when he heads into the office or has a meeting like this one. I can't help swooning at him. He's suited and booted in a dark navy three-piece suit, a white shirt, and a dark grey tie. He shouldn't look this good – and I wonder for a second how many women are going to be gawking at him throughout the meetings he's going to have.

Tristan smiles a little sadly at me, making my heart ache. He's going to miss me like I'm going to miss him. I feel the tears bubble to the surface but push them back. The last thing I want is to make Tristan feel bad for leaving me. It's just a business trip.

He'll be home on Wednesday, and I definitely don't want him to drive away with the image of me blubbering away like an idiot.

"Baby, did you want to stay in bed or say goodbye downstairs?" he softly asks.

I swallow hard as my heart constricts hearing him say that. My stomach turns and flips, making me feel nauseous, and once again I fight back the urge to cry.

"No," I answer groggily and push the covers away. "I want to see you off," I add.

"Edith's made you a Cappuccino," he says, gesturing to the cup sitting on the bedside cabinet - *Sweet Edith, I shall miss her too.*

I nod and smile at Tristan as I slide out of bed. I glance at his bags that are ready and packed as I head into the en-suite, instantly wishing I hadn't done, because the feeling of loss that I haven't felt since I married Tristan, rears its ugly head. I try to push the feeling away as I clean my teeth and wash my face, but it's not working, and once again I try to work out why it is that I'm feeling so strange about him leaving, as he has done before, but I get no definitive answer.

Taking a deep breath, I pull on my winter robe and open the bathroom door, and there he is, sitting on the edge of the bed, looking amazing, and sexy, and very powerful and important. He holds his hand out to me, and without a second thought, I run towards him, place my hand in his, and he pulls me down, knowing exactly what I want, and I curl up on his lap, inhaling deeply.

"This sucks," he says, making me smile because those are not the words you expect to hear from the mouth of a man dressed so smartly, who is extremely intelligent and can speak very eloquently when he wants to.

"Yeah..." I breathe – feeling lighter for him saying that.

"Still wish you would come with me," he whispers, squeezing me tight.

"I've got to take Bob to the Dr's today," I remind him.

"I know," he replies, 'but later, when you're done, you can always get Danny to drive you to London to be with me, or get the train," he adds.

And I realise that's not a bad idea. "If I feel...weird I will," I tell him.

We stay like that for a while, just holding one another.

"Time to go," he softly says with a kiss on the top of my head.

"Ok," I croak, then look up and place my hand on his cheek. "I'll miss you," I whisper, and the tears come, even though I don't want them to.

"Oh baby," he croons, 'I'll miss you too." His lips reach mine, and I can feel the ache behind his kiss. He pulls back and smiles warmly at me. "Come on, the sooner I'm gone, the sooner I'll be back," he softly says.

I smile up at him, and slide of his lap. "You'll call me when you get there?" I ask as he places his hand in mine and stands.

"You know I will," he tells me, then releasing my hand he picks up his overnight bag, and his briefcase, and taking my hand again, we walk silently down the stairs, and into the living area.

Edith is sitting on the sofa with her bags next to her, and my heart constricts again. Releasing Tristan's hand, I dash over to Edith, who stands as I approach her, and then we are hugging.

"I'm going to really miss you," I manage to croak. *Stupid fucking tears!*

"Oh sweetheart, I'll miss you too," Edith whispers back.

I release her from the hug and feeling silly for crying, I manage to smile. "Have a wonderful Christmas," I say, sniffing once.

Edith smiles widely at me. "And you too," she says, and surprising me, she tucks my hair behind my ear. "If you need me, just call ok," she adds.

I nod once, as I have lost the power of speech.

"Right then, I'll wait for you in the car," she says to Tristan, who is dropping her off at the train station, and I watch with a heavy heart as Edith picks up her bags and heads down the stairs to the lower floor.

I turn to Tristan, trying my best to keep it together and smile widely at him. But he looks just as cut up about leaving as I do. I swallow hard against the lump that's formed. Then Tristan walks over to me, and taking my hand in his, we silently head down to the garage. Danny has been down here getting everything ready for Tristan and has already started the car, warming up the engine, and Edith is waiting in the passenger seat.

"Everything checked?" Tristan asks him, as Danny takes his bags off him and places them in the boot.

"Yes Sir," Danny replies.

"Good. You know what to do," Tristan says to Danny in a tone that's not to be argued with.

"Yes," Danny replies and shakes Tristan's hand. "You can rely on me," he adds.

And I have to wonder what that was all about.

Danny then nods to me and walks away. I start shivering. And I'm not sure if it's because it's so cold down here, or because Tristan is about to leave. My teeth clench together as I realise the moment I have been dreading has finally come.

"Hey," Tristan says, wrapping me up in his arms. "You're getting cold Coral."

"It's cold in here," I manage to croak.

Reaching down he tips my chin up and gently plants his lips on mine. "Be good," he says, 'do what Danny tells you to do, and don't get doing anything heroic," he adds with a chuckle.

This makes me smile. I jump up and wrap my arms around his neck, squeezing him tightly. "Be safe in this weather won't you," I whisper.

"Always," he tells me.

I let go and slide down his body, which kinks his tie, so I reach up and put it back in place for him. "Go get em, baby," I say with a wink, which makes him smile too.

"I will," he says, and with one last kiss, he lets me go and gets into the car.

I wrap my arms around myself as I watch the electronic garage door open, and Tristan pulling out onto the driveway. He presses the button in the Jag to close the door again, and I wave to them both, and they both wave back at me, and I feel like I'm going to throw up. *Keep it together Coral!*

With one last wave, he disappears from view, and the hum of the garage door closing stops, and all I can hear is silence. Not liking the way that's making me feel, I run out of the garage and all the way up the stairs until I reach our bedroom - and he's still here in the room. I can feel him and smell him, which just makes me feel even more sorry for myself, the ache in my stomach growing stronger by the second. I crawl up onto the bed, grab hold of his pillow, which smells just like him, hug it to me, and begin to silently weep...

I STAND WITH my arms crossed, glaring angrily at Bob. After a very thorough checkup by Dr Andrews, he has been put on bed rest. Turns out he hasn't got a cold he's got a virus, which he is on antibiotics for, because of his age. And he's not supposed to be doing anything – but will he listen, oh no! After trying to convince him in the car that I want him to come and stay with

## A Christmas Wish

Tristan and me until he's better, and utterly failing, I have driven him to Gladys' so she can try and talk some sense into him.

"Bob...sweetheart," Gladys softly says. "You must stay with one of us," she adds.

Bob huffs and crosses his arms in defiance.

"Bob," I say in a firm tone. "You have two choices, Gladys' or mine!"

"Coral, sweetheart," Gladys says, and subtly shakes her head at me, and I know she means to calm down. "I think Bob just feels' – "I'll stay here," Bob interrupts.

I can't help huffing at him. "And what's wrong with staying with me?" I ask. And I know it's because the house is already feeling strange and quiet without Tristan and Edith.

Bob turns to me and begins to smile. "I remember what it's like being a newlywed," he says, wiggling his eyebrows up and down – *Holy crap!*

My mouth pops open. "Bob!"

"Well it's true," he says.

"Gladys is a newlywed too," I bite back. *She's probably bonking Malcolm more than I am Tristan!*

"Yes, but it's different when you're younger, right?" Bob argues, looking up at her.

Gladys' cheeks start to pink, but she nods her head seriously as she agrees with Bob. "Of course!" she says, and glances once at me – and I can't help the sarcastic look I give her.

"Fine!" I bark, feeling mad it won't be with me.

Gladys glares at me in a way that I know is telling me off – *Fuck!*

I sigh heavily, then walk over to Bob and kneel down in front of him. "You're really going to stay here and let Gladys look after you?" I softly ask.

"Yes," he sighs – He hates this, I know.

"And you'll do what she says?" I ask.

Bob frowns down at me. "Yes," he grumpily replies.

Tears spring to my eyes. "Thank you," I whisper, feeling my shoulders coming down from my ears.

"Don't worry Bob, we'll get you set up in the spare room with a T.V and radio, so you'll still have your independence, or if you want to, you can be with Malcolm and me," Gladys cheerily says.

Bob perks up a little bit. "Thanks, Gladdie," he replies – For some reason, he's always called her that.

"Ok then," I breathe. "I'll go and get your prescription, and anything you need from your studio."

"Sounds like a plan," Gladys adds with a smile. And so I go, back to Bobs with his list of things that he needs.

AN HOUR LATER, I am sat in George's office drinking a cup of tea. After sorting Bob out with what he needed, and my mind at rest that he's in good hands, my thoughts have been of Tristan, and only Tristan. He did call me earlier to say he had arrived safely, and the meeting was already underway, which I am grateful for, but I guess I just wanted to hear his voice for a little while longer.

"How are you Coral?" George asks.

"I'm good thanks, you?" I ask.

George smiles fondly at me. "Very well indeed," he replies.

"Great!" I say, smiling broadly at him.

George raises an eyebrow at me, and he's looking over the rim of his glasses in that way of his. I sigh heavily and wrap my hands around my teacup.

"I'm not here for a session George," I tell him. I only see George once every couple of weeks now, and I'm not due here until next week.

"I know," he replies, still staring at me in that way of his – he knows something is up.

I huff in annoyance and look up at him. "Fine! - I'm freaking out!" I say, feeling angry at myself. My leg starts jigging up and down, a sure sign of anxiety – *Ugh!*

"About?" George prompts.

"Tristan being away," I reply, my voice shaking on me.

"Ah..." George leans forward and removes his glasses. "And were you feeling this way on the other occasions he has been away?"

I shake my head and take a sip of tea.

"I see," he says.

"You do?" I squeak, 'because I can't get my head around it, George. This is the third time he's been away in the two months since...well, you know, and I just don't understand it. I was fine before," I say, feeling anxious about it all again. "Besides, I came here for a different reason, I know I'm just being silly about Tristan," I look up at him. "I think talking about it will just make it worse, if that makes sense?" I add, frowning at myself.

George smiles at me. "Alright then," he says, and takes a sip of tea, waiting for me to speak.

I take a deep breath. "I'm hosting Christmas this year, and

## A Christmas Wish

I wanted to invite you and Phil over," I say, without any hope, as every time I have built myself up, it's all come crashing down on me.

"Oh, lovely!" George replies.

I look up at him, eyes wide, not really sure if I heard him right.

"We'd love to," George adds.

"Don't you need to check with Phil first?" I ask.

George chuckles once. "No need, the friends we were supposed to be spending it with have had a family emergency," he says, 'so I know we are completely free," George adds.

"Great!" I beam, feeling excited. "So it will be Christmas Eve for cocktails and party snacks, and then Christmas Day lunch?" I ask.

"Sounds wonderful," George smiles. "But don't you think it may be a little too much?" he adds.

I roll my eyes at him. "You sound like Tristan," I grumble.

"He may have a point," George replies – *Ugh!*

My foot starts tapping in annoyance. "I want to show my family and friends how much I love them. I want to somehow, make up for all the years I've lost by being...me, and this is the way in which I want to do it," I say.

"I understand," George replies. And I know he's holding something back.

I narrow my eyes at him. "Say what's on your mind George," I blurt out.

George nods once and thinks about it for a second. "The fact that you want to do this denotes some guilt on your part for simply being who you are, or, who you were. And you shouldn't be feeling guilty Coral, at all. We all have our crosses to bear, and it's not like you weren't trying to better yourself, in-fact, I've never known any patient work so hard on improving themselves. And I worry that if it doesn't all go according to plan, this *'I'm sorry please forgive me Christmas dinner'* that it may set you back because you have such high expectations for it."

I frown at the cup in my hand. "You don't need to worry about that George, hardly anyone is coming," I say, then proceed to tell him all about my invites, and all of the declines.

"Oh dear," George softly says in sympathy.

"Yeah..." I grumble. "But at least you and Phil are coming," I say, feeling decidedly better for it.

George narrows his eyes at me. "Can I ask you something Coral?"

I swallow hard, knowing it's probably going to be something profound and deep, as it usually is with George. "Ok," I squeak, which makes George chuckle.

He then takes a moment to compose himself, and with a furrowed brow, he looks me dead in the eye. "Do you think, that there's some part of you, that you may not have acknowledged, or even realise is there, that is pushing you to have this big family Christmas because you're afraid of being on your own with Tristan?" He asks, with his hands folded together in front of him. *What the fuck!*

"I'm not afraid of Tristan!" I balk.

"You misunderstand me," George says with his hands held up. 'What I meant to say is, do you think there's a possibility that there is an underlying fear of being on your own with him at this time of year, at Christmas? It sounds to me like you're putting a lot of pressure on yourself to make him happy, and maybe, on some subliminal level, you feel as though you may not be enough if it were just the two of you, or that he'll be disappointed in you somehow?"

I frown back at him and ponder the question. "I don't think so," I whisper, wondering if George is right. "I wanted to do this for us both. On my part, so I could spoil my family and friends who have been there for Tristan and me, and then also for Tristan too. He lost his folks, and in a way has no family of his own left, and I wanted to show him that he does have a family, a big one, that loves him just as much as I do," I say.

George smiles warmly at me. "That's lovely Coral," he says.

My mouth pops open. "That's it?" I balk. "You put those thoughts into my head about fear and not being good enough, and expect me to forget them?" I say, my eyebrows raised.

George slowly shakes his head once from side to side. And I realise what he's doing. Maybe he can see it, even though I can't, and I'm not even sure if I am holding out on Tristan because I'm afraid?

"Ok," I say, nodding my head several times, 'Food for thought?" I question.

George nods his head once. *Hmm...Am I doing it because I'm afraid of not being enough?*

"Coral!" Phil shouts as he comes barging into the room. Reaching me, he air kisses both my cheeks and takes a seat next to me. "It's been ages!" he says, his voice high pitched.

"I know," I giggle, glancing once at George, letting him

know its ok Phil interrupted us. It wasn't like we were actually having a session.

"Coral has invited us over for Christmas," George tells Phil.

His face drops. "Well that's lovely darling, but don't you remember we promised we would see my sister this year if it fell through with the Kellermans?"

George slaps the heel of his hand to his forehead. "And so we did," he says, but I notice a funny squeak come from Phil, and glance across at him, to find he's rapidly winking at George.

"Ok!" I laugh, getting to my feet. "I saw that what's going on Phil?"

He turns and looks up at me, blinking rapidly. "I think I have something in my eye!" he squeaks, and dashes out of the room.

I look down at George, who shakes his head in bewilderment. "I often wonder how it is that we ever fell in love," he says, still shaking his head.

I cross my arms in defiance. He's not getting away with it that easily. "What am I missing here George?" I ask my foot starts to join in, tapping away.

George looks me dead in the eye again. "*You* are not missing a thing," George laughs, 'it's Phil I'm worried about, a sandwich short of a picnic that one!"

And I know he's just teasing, he loves Phil to bits, but that's not the point here. I smile down at him, but my eyes are still narrowed, I don't believe a word he is saying, something is going on.

George suddenly points a finger up in the air. "I've got it!" he says.

"You have?" I laugh, hoping he's about to share the secret.

"When is your period is due?" He asks – *What?*

"What?" I ask, feeling as though it's the oddest question he's ever asked.

"When is it due?" He asks again.

I sit back down and frown back at him as I try to work it out. "Um...in about a week I think," I whisper, feeling a little embarrassed.

George nods to himself. "Coral, this may sound strange to you, but I always knew during the time we spent together when your period was due," he looks up at me, and I frown back at him. "Forgive me," he says, 'it's just that when it was, you would always be...more on edge, more anxious," he says.

I stare back at him, knowing he's trying to tell me something, but what I don't know.

"Maybe that's why you're feeling anxious about Tristan being away?" he softly implies.

*Oh, holy crap!*

And I realise he's right – I do get more anxious around that time, it's only natural, but it certainly explains my weird, melancholy feelings. And I'm sure if I check the calendar on my phone, it will show I wasn't due when Tristan went away before, which would make perfect sense.

"George, you are a bloody lifesaver!" I gasp. "I was starting to think something bad was going to happen to him, and I wasn't picking up on it properly and..." I stop and shake my head with a little laugh. "Thanks, George, I feel a lot better now," I add.

He smiles warmly at me. "That's what I'm here for," he says and stands with his arms open wide.

I hug him. "Thanks, George," I whisper.

He pats my back then smiles up at me. "I am sorry we can't make it for Christmas. I was looking forward to it," he says with absolute sincerity. Which makes me think Phil's odd behaviour was just that, Phil – being odd.

And then I realise that it's another decline. Maybe it really isn't meant to be? I sigh inwardly and then frown as I re-think what George just said about subconsciously avoiding being alone with Tristan. So I have to ask - *Am I avoiding it?*

"George - Help!" Phil squeals down the hallway, making George roll his eyes.

"You better go see him," I laugh, 'I'll see myself out," I add.

"Sure?" George asks I nod, so we give each other a goodbye kiss. I head out of their house and begin driving home, back to a dark, empty house named Seascape.

A house without Tristan.

# NINE

Tristan

I'M IN THE X-J, driving home to Brighton, to Coral, my darling wife who I have missed so badly in the two nights and three days I have been away from her. There's another storm raging, so I have kept my speed down, and been more careful, as Coral has asked me to. I glance at the time again – 11.45pm. I'm late, much later than I said I would be; which I am not pleased about. I hate being late. Especially with Coral, she'll worry, which makes me worry. *Concentrate Tristan!*

Its pitch black outside, rain pounding against the windscreen, the wipers on full blast, but the Jag can take it and is effortlessly eating up the miles. Yet, this journey that I have made many times now feels like it's taking forever. I know it's because I am desperate to be home, at Seascape, with Coral.

I finally see the lights of Brighton City in the distance and feel a sense of relief wash over me. I focus on the black, slick road ahead as The Verve sing Lucky Man to me. And as I hum along to the tune, I have to agree. I am one lucky man.

Out of nowhere, I get a flashback of a melancholy feeling that wouldn't leave me this time last year. A loneliness like I can never explain as my first Christmas without my folks approached. I clench my teeth as I think about how bad it was. The waves of grief that filled my mind and body, day after day, were relentless. That Christmas was horrendous. I never want to feel like that again.

I try to shake off the memories by thinking about this year, and how different it's going to be. There are less than three weeks to go until Christmas, and surprisingly, I'm feeling good about it. I've had my moments and will continue to have them. And even though I wish my folks were still here, it hasn't hurt as much as it did last year.

I know that's because I have Coral now.

She has filled my life with love and happiness. I no longer feel alone. I smile widely at that thought. Then I think about how much she has changed me, how much she has grown, and how much has happened since we met less than six short months ago. But all is well now. Life is pleasant here at Seascape. Coral is happy. I am happy and in love.

As I continue to drive, and really wanting to put my foot down so I can get to Coral, an old memory begins to replay of my folks. It's one of my most memorable because everything my folks said that day has come true. And as I think back on that night we spent together, I can't help thinking how right they both were with what they told me, and how much I wish they could both see how happy I now am...

IT WAS A REGULAR Wednesday evening. I was quiet and contemplative, I had been for the past month since the end of my relationship with Olivia. I wasn't in a talkative mood. I could tell Granny and Gramps were worried, which only added pressure as I didn't want to worry them. I was in a funk that I couldn't seem to pull myself out of.

"You'll find her one day Tristan, that special girl," Granny said, surprising me.

Gramps kept quiet. He always did when Granny was dishing out advice. This was not a conversation I wanted to have. But they'd raised me to be respectful of them, so I played along.

I tried a smile. "You think so?" I questioned.

"Yes." She was absolutely positive. "When the time is right, she'll come into your life at exactly the right time and the right place."

"How can you be so sure?" I asked.

"Because that's how it works. When you're ready, and she's ready, you'll meet. And she'll be everything you ever wanted, and you'll be everything she ever wanted." She told me, I could see she believed in what she was saying to me. And a part of me hoped it was true.

"I hope you're right Granny," I replied.

"I know I'm right," she told me and squeezed my hand. Then she gave me one of her most loving, adoring smiles. "Tristan, you are a wonderful man, so loving and sweet. You haven't changed since you were a boy, and I am so very proud of you, of how hard you have worked, and how much you have achieved. And one day, the right girl will come along and appreciate all those things about you too, and love you unconditionally for it."

I felt guilt-ridden. Had I spent enough time with them? Had I done was I was supposed to have done, or what I thought I should do?

"Are you happy Granny?" I asked.

"Yes, darling. I have your Grandpa, and I have you. I don't need anything else."

I nodded and glanced across at Gramps. "And you Gramps?"

Gramps frowned at me and contemplated for a moment. "Son, we've never told you this, but we tried for years to fall pregnant, didn't we Rose." He looked to Granny, and she smiled at him. "Yes Freddie, we did."

"Went to see the doctor," he continued. "Told us it might not happen, there was no way to check up on these things back then, so we resigned ourselves to the probability that it may never happen. And then Rose was sick, and I was scared stupid. I thought I might lose her. Turned out she'd fallen pregnant with your mother. We were delighted. Although Granny had it tough, didn't you darling."

Granny smiled again. "Oh, the worst pregnancy in the history of the world, I swear!"

"And then little Beth was born, healthy as a horse. We were so happy and enjoyed being parents, but we didn't want to go through all that again. So we were resigned, one child, no more. We would cherish and love her and give her everything we could. And then we had the pleasure of your mother falling pregnant with you. We were looking forward to being Grandparents weren't we Rose."

"Yes darling, we even started a saving account for you." Granny touched my cheek tenderly.

Gramps was quiet for a moment, shook his head, stared down at the table and then continued in a low voice. "Worse thing in the world to lose your child, no matter what age they are, there ain't no other feeling like it. And it stays with you for as long as you live."

I stopped breathing. My mother was rarely mentioned. I always thought it was because they didn't want to upset me, but now I could see it was because it was so hard for them to remember. Granny's eyes filled with tears. I took her hand in mine and held on tight.

"Life is cruel sometimes," Gramps continued. "Rose and I were devastated, we were never going to see Beth again, enjoy her smile, or her infectious giggling, or have her hug us so hard we had to tell her to let go. She was such a sweet, loving girl..." Gramps turned away, unable to continue.

Granny looked at me and smiled, then continued as Gramps seemed to be struggling.

"God also blessed us by giving us you." She softly said. "Every time we looked at you, we saw your mother. We saw her smile, heard her laugh, felt her loving us through you. And for that, we will always be truly grateful." She told me.

I nodded, not sure of what to say.

"Ask me again son." Gramps prompted, his voice gruff, I could tell he was emotional, and I knew what he meant.

I choked back the lump in my throat. "Are you happy Gramps?"

"More than you can ever know. I am just as proud of you, and I love you, son," he answered then he reached forward, cupped me around the neck and gave me an awkward man hug. Gramps quickly released me, as Granny was always the more affectionate one, but I felt the need to let them both know how much they meant to me too.

"I hope you both know that you mean the world to me. If you hadn't have raised me, god knows where I would have been. I love you both. I just want you to know that."

"We know Tristan," Granny said. "Yes, we know that son," Gramps added.

We all smiled at one another, then laughed, and as the evening drew on, Granny retired early, and Gramps and I continued the game of chess that we'd been playing on and off for several weeks now.

I poured myself a Brandy, and Gramps a Whiskey then sat opposite him.

"Something you need to know son." He looked dead serious.

"I'm all ears," I told him.

"I knew the moment I met your Granny that she was the one, just one look from across the dance floor, and I was a goner. I knew, right there and then that I wanted to spend the rest of my life staring into her eyes."

I didn't really get his point. "I know you love her Gramps," I sighed.

He shook his head at me. "You're not listening."

I frowned at him. "Yes, I am."

He sighed and took a sip of Whiskey. "Did you feel like that when you met Olivia?"

I laughed. "Er...no Gramps. We didn't really have that kind of relationship."

He cocked an eyebrow. "What, you saying it was just sex for three years?"

Kinky, dark, fucking, that's what it was - I laughed again, feeling a little uncomfortable we were having this conversation. "Something like that," I replied.

He shook his head in disapproval and started mumbling to himself, which always annoyed me.

"What?" I pushed.

He took another sip of Whiskey. "I don't understand what you were doing with someone like her, I liked that other one!"

"What other one?" I asked, surprised by his sudden outburst.

"April." He looked sternly at me. "Reminded me of your Granny that girl did."

I froze, staring back at him in utter shock. He remembered her name. "Gramps, I didn't even know you remembered her' – "Well, of course, I remember her!" He interrupted, more passionately now.

I stayed quiet. I hadn't thought of April, my first and only teenage love, in a very long time.

"Look, son, there's all kinds of people in the world, and I've tried to toughen you up' – "Wait, are you saying I'm not tough?" I barked back.

"No!" he glared at me then, and I fell silent. "That is not what I'm saying. You're smart Tristan. Tough when you have to be, but intellectuals generally don't go around with a cocky chip on their shoulder. Tough guys do, and you my son, are not one of them. I know you, Tristan. You're a carbon copy of your mother. You have all her attributes, thoughtfulness, kindness, empathy for others, all the traits that make you who you are. What I'm trying to say to you is this – You're too nice, which isn't a bad thing. Just stop allowing the wrong kind of women to come into your life. Make a stand for yourself. Don't enter into another relationship unless you know she's just as invested in you as you are in her. Don't let another one like Olivia use you, Tristan."

It was the longest speech I'd ever heard him make.

"Do you understand what I'm saying?" He asked in a firm tone.

I nodded once. He was right. But I didn't want to talk about it – I was still too pissed at myself and Olivia to be thinking about anyone new coming into my life. In fact, I didn't want anyone new.

"Say it out loud," he prompted.

I sighed heavily. "Yes, Gramps. I get it. I get what you're saying."

"Good. If you think like that, then you will find the right girl does come along. It doesn't mean it's going to be easy though because if it's easy, it ain't worth fighting for. Tougher it is, harder you have to fight for her, and the more you'll mean to each other. That's how it was with your Granny and me, we fought all the time and loved all the time. One date was all it took, and I knew my life would never be complete without her. So don't pursue it unless you feel like that about her, ok?"

A part of me wanted to laugh at him. Gramps had never really given me advice about women before, more like commented here and there. But as I really absorbed what he'd said, I knew he was right, and I knew I wanted to feel that way about a girl – well, one day.

"You have my word, Gramps. I understand." I smiled at him.

He smiled at me, leaned forward, and we clinked glasses.

"Tristan look," he pointed down to the chess table with a wicked gleam in his eyes.

I looked down, Gramps had won – *Damn it!*

I'd been so busy listening to his speech, I hadn't seen his move. But that didn't mean I couldn't try to beat him all over again...

THE CHRISTMAS LIGHTS hanging above me as I cruise the car through Brighton town centre make me smile to myself, and I wonder if Coral and I should go out over the next couple of days and enjoy them. In fact, the more I think about it, the more I realise I haven't really helped Coral with any Christmas shopping. She – no, I shouldn't think like that – we have a big family, including friends to buy gifts for, and I really should be helping her with that. I nod my head in agreement with myself and turn left into our driveway. All the outdoor Christmas lights are on that Danny, and I put up on Sunday.

In the middle of the round lawn is the glowing Snowman, and right next to the front door is the glowing Father Christmas that Coral loved, me not so much, which makes me chuckle to myself as I remember Coral's face lighting up when she realised what they were.

My crazy, beautiful, girl.

Finally - I am home. I feel a sense of relief as I switch off the engine. The drive from London was tiring. I collect my bag and briefcase from the boot of the car, lock her up and head towards the front door, excited to see Coral, and glad to be back in Brighton.

I walk into the house, expecting to see Coral come running towards me, her eyes filled with love and adoration for me. One of the many things I love about that woman is that she's always so genuinely pleased to see me, as I am her. I've never had that before, a woman who truly loves me for who I am. And as tired as I am, I can't wait to lose myself in her, to feel her soft skin against mine, have her wonderful, sexy, naked body wrapped around mine as I bury myself deep inside her.

I imagine waking up beside her in the morning, neither of us having to be anywhere. In fact, I think it's a damn good idea to spend the day in bed. We have a lot of catching up to do. The thought makes me so hard, my dick actually aches. *Down boy, later!*

As I punch in the code for the alarm, I notice the time. It's late, 12.15am. The drive took a lot longer than anticipated with the bad weather. Scanning the room, I notice the only light is coming from the low lights in the kitchen, and the Christmas Tree sat in the corner by the fire. The stereo is on - Chris Rea's Driving Home For Christmas is playing.

I frown to myself as I lock the front door, and re-alarm the house. Coral did say she was going to wait up for me, as she always does, and she's always kept her word. I wonder for a moment if I have done something wrong, or not done something, but then I hear her whimper, and I know what it means.

I drop my bag and briefcase to the floor and go in search of her.

My heart has picked up its pace. It's my usual reaction to hearing that noise. Coral is dreaming, having a nightmare. She doesn't always tell me what they are about – and I'm guessing those are the really bad ones – but sometimes she does. I have talked to George about this, as I was naive enough to believe that once we were married and settled, they would have stopped, but as George reminded me, this is her way of coping with things, and he doesn't believe that her mind will ever stop being so active.

They are not as frequent as they used to be, and always seem to occur when I've been away. I have argued this point with Coral, that she should come with me when I have to travel, but she insists on staying here, citing time apart is just as important as quality time together. *'How are we ever supposed to have the opportunity to miss one another?'* she stated, and in a way, I know she is right.

I just miss her so damn much. My argumentative, troublesome girl who I completely and utterly love and adore – she whimpers again, bringing me back to the now.

I pick up my pace down the hallway, knowing she is in pain. But then her whimpering changes to something more sinister and more gut-wrenching. Just as I reach the edge of the sofa, I realise she's not there, it makes my stomach turn. *Where are you?*

"Coral?" I call out, hoping her subconscious will recognise my voice and she'll respond – which she does – with an earth-shattering scream that chills me to the bone.

Instantly realising where it's coming from, I dash into the library and find Coral on the sofa, her body curled up into a tense, rigid ball. Her hands are tight fists above her head, and her breathing has skyrocketed. *Oh my love, my darling...*

This is why I hate leaving her so much.

I kneel down in front of her, and gently stroke her cheek. "Wake up my love, you're dreaming..." I whisper. I feel so helpless. I want to shake her awake, so I can stop her going through this pain, but the first time I did that, I made it worse, and I almost ended up with a black eye. George advised me that from now on, a gentle approach is what's needed, and he's right, it works better this way.

I lean towards her, place my hand over her clenched fist and whisper in her ear. "Wake up my darling. I am home. You're safe now, wake up."

Her breathing starts to slow, and the tension in her muscles subsides a little, a small whimper escapes her lips – clenching my heart as it does – I wish I could take it all away for her.

"Can you hear me, baby? It's Tristan. I am home my love, you are safe. Wake up if you want to darling." Her eyes dart open and meet mine, they are wide and full of fear, and I wait for her to do or say whatever is necessary to make her feel better, sometimes she's very disorientated when she wakes.

"Tristan..." she chokes out as tears spill over and roll down her cheeks. "You're home."

"Yes. I'm here my love," I say as I stroke her cheek again. "You're safe now."

Without a word, she scrambles into my arms, and I know that whatever the dream was, it scared her. As we sit on the sofa, Coral on my lap, curled up in my arms like a helpless child, I wait for the sweats and shaking to begin, which normally do after a bad dream. She clutches me so tightly, her head buried beneath my chin, as she begins to softly weep.

"Shh, it's ok baby. It was just a bad dream," I try to soothe her, kissing the top of her head, and stroking her back.

"I know," she whimpers, clutching me tighter.

"Just a silly dream my love, I've got you. You're ok now." Her weeping slowly subsides as I gently rock her, and then she looks up at me, her eyes slightly bloodshot.

"I'm sorry," she whispers.

"For what baby?" I softly ask as I wipe a tear away with my thumb.

"I fell asleep," she whimpers again, her face full of remorse.

"Coral' – I'm about to scorn her for being so silly, but she knows I'm about to do exactly that and interrupts me – "Don't tell me I'm being silly Tristan...please don't. I let you down." She sniffs a couple of times and hangs her head in shame.

"And look what happened because I did fall asleep...you come home to this..." Her bottom lip begins to tremble. "It's not much of a welcome home is it?"

"Oh, my love..." Ignoring her pleading for wanting to feel guilty, I crush her to me, kissing her head several times. "What am I going to do with you?" I chuckle.

"Don't know what you *are* doing with me..." she replies, and I know she means it.

This makes me mad.

"Enough Coral! I won't hear you saying things like that. I love you, I need you, and I want you, for the rest of my life. Why do you think I married you?" I ask.

"I don't know..." she mumbles.

I sigh inwardly at that reply. Sometimes the dreams make her feel like this, they play on her fears, as they do for all of us, but they seem to affect her so much more, and I know she finds them hard to shake off. The last time she had a really bad dream, which she didn't want to talk about, she walked around in a daze for the rest of the day, she was trying not to, but I could tell, I could see the difference.

"I'm so sorry," she croaks and sinks her head beneath my chin again.

"Coral, listen to me. Coming home to find you having a nightmare isn't a bad thing you know. You haven't let me down at all. If anything it makes my heart ache for you darling, I want to take it all away for you. Have the nightmares for you. I'd kick the shit out of anyone that tries to hurt or frighten you."

This makes her chuckle.

"I just want to comfort you, baby, make you feel safe," I add and kiss her head again.

"Oh Tristan, you do make me feel safe," she croaks, squeezing me tighter. "I love you so much, you know that right?"

I smile outwardly and inwardly. Hearing her say those words always warms me from the inside out. I don't think that will ever change.

"Yes, I know darling, as I love you." I tip her back, and she looks up at me, reaches up and gently strokes my cheek.

"Kiss me," she whispers. I lean down and do exactly that. And it's such a sweet, loving kiss that she gives back to me, I can tell she's missed me, as I have her.

"Better now?" I whisper against her lips.

She nods once, so I know she's not.

"Want to talk about it?" I ask, hesitantly.

She takes a deep breath. "It was Kane."

Just hearing that name is all it takes to fire me up. I feel my cheeks flush red, and I know my eyes will have darkened with anger and hate for the pond scum that he is. And it kills me that even though he's dead, he's still here, frightening the shit out of my wife through her dreams.

"That fucker!" I hiss through gritted teeth.

"Tristan..." Her voice is calm.

I swallow hard and take a deep breath trying to regain my composure. "I apologise, I just hate the thought of him hurting you, even in your dreams."

Coral takes another deep breath. "It wasn't anything new," she whispers.

I look down at her. "Nothing new?"

"It was...you know... what happened in the pool room that day." Her eyes close for a moment.

I frown at her. I can't tell if she's just saying that to protect

## A Christmas Wish

me. "You screamed Coral, a terrible scream, it made my blood curdle." I feel a shiver run down my spine.

"That was probably the part where you wouldn't wake up, I couldn't resuscitate you," she whimpers.

I reach out and stroke her cheek. "So it wasn't Kane trying to hurt you?" I ask - I have to know.

"No baby. Not Kane. The only person in the world that can hurt me now is you, so you better stick around hubby." She grins widely at me, and I know my girl is back. "I'm sorry," she says again.

"Seriously Coral, if you apologise once more' – "You'll what?" she asks, her eyes wide and teasing.

"I'll take you over my knee," I tell her playfully.

"Oooh...I like the sound of that," she giggles.

"Oh really?" I tease back, laughing too.

"Yes," she giggles in delight, so I lean down and kiss her, she reciprocates, her tongue swimming passionately against mine.

I moan with want as I move her so that she's straddling me, our lips still entwined.

"Wait!" Coral suddenly stops and pulls back, we are both panting.

"What baby?" I ask, running my hands up her legs, noticing for the first time that she's wearing a very sexy, short, black lingerie piece. That her makeup is dark and smoky and very sexy, and she's done something different with her hair, making it look wild and sexy like Julia Roberts in Pretty Woman – I had a thing for her back in the day.

Coral rests her hands against my cheeks. "Aren't you hungry? Thirsty?" she asks, her eyes searching mine – Oh yeah, and she smells fucking amazing!

"Only for you," I whisper, my dick throbbing against her.

"Oh Tristan," she whispers, 'I have missed you so." She leans her forehead against mine with her eyes closed.

"I've missed you too baby. I want you – now!" I tell her, inhaling her sweet scent.

"So take me," she teases - I don't think twice.

Finding the hem of her lingerie, I slowly lift it across her backside, up over her torso, until her breast are free, the satin feels smooth and sexy, making my dick pound even harder, I pull it over her shoulders and throw it onto the floor. Noticing the very skimpy black thong, she has on – *Damn she drives me wild!*

I reach down and sink my mouth around her pert nipple.

Her eyes close and she moans in delight, making me want to be buried in her right now.

"Tristan," she whispers, 'in me, right now," she pants.

Great minds think alike. I reach down, wishing I wasn't wearing my suit, click the belt open, the button and the zip on my trousers, as Coral quickly relinquishes me of my tie and unbuttons my shirt, her hands running across my chest and abdomen – *Fuck I want her, so badly!*

"Coral," I moan and kiss her again.

"Oh Tristan, you turn me on so much baby!" She pants, kissing me harder, faster. Little moans of pleasure escaping her lips. I lean up and pull my trousers and boxers down. My dick springs free, hard and aching, ready to rock. Coral cups him in her hand and slowly moves up and down, watching her own handy work. *Fuck, she's good at this.*

I look up at her, she looks down at me – and I'm consumed by the amount of love I have for this girl. That feeling in my abdomen swells and flows through me, filling every corner of my being.

I skim my hand up the inside of her thigh until I reach her soft, warm, wet, and very inviting clit. I circle my fingers around a couple of times, making her moan, her hand falters against my dick. Not wanting to waste any more time, I lift and position her, she slowly pushes down on me until I'm full to the brim, buried deep inside her, just like I wanted to be earlier.

"Oh baby...the way you make me feel," I tell her. I can never fully explain it, not in words.

"Ditto baby," she moans and begins to move.

Reaching down, she takes my face in her hands and sinks her tongue into my mouth, moving in time with her hips. I'm overwhelmed. This woman, this beautiful, fragile soul is my wife. I still have to pinch myself sometimes that it's true - I wrap my arms tightly around her, pulling her closer to me, and lose myself in her beautiful, sexy warmth...

# TEN

I WAKE AND REALISE we're still in the same position we fell asleep in. I'm on my side, Tristan is behind me with his strong forearms wrapped around me, his one hand holding mine, his other resting on my arm. Our legs are entwined, and his head is gently resting against mine with his lips resting against my shoulder. I very slowly turn my head so I can peek at him, he looks so lovely, and just as I think that he takes a deep, satisfied breath, gives me a squeeze with his arms, and breathes out, falling back into his deep slumber.

I'm so happy he's home. I close my eyes again, feeling deeply relaxed and in love. His scent surrounds me, so I take another deep breath as he softly sleeps beside me. Oh, I love this, and I have missed him terribly, even though he's only been gone for a couple of days. As I slowly come back down to earth, I look up at the clock on the wall, only to find its almost 2pm. Tristan and I have spent the whole day in bed, making love, talking and giggling like a couple of teenagers that are up to no good, which ironically was not only my plan but Tristan's too.

I sigh, feeling blissfully happy. It's absolutely bucketing down outside, rain lashing hard against the windows, the wind is howling, and it's so dark already. There's supposed to be another storm on its way. Yet, lying here, I feel warm, safe, and happy.

I glance down at the Christmas Tree lights that are twinkling sweetly, and I can't help thinking of those that don't have this. I mean a roof over their heads. I always think of the homeless this time of year, of how cold and hungry they must be. Maybe that's because it was almost my predicament, or maybe it's because Christmas is supposed to be the time of year that one thinks of others, and helps others. Yet like most things it has become commercialised along with everything else, which is annoying

- But for now, I will clear my mind and enjoy this blissful moment with my lovely husband.

My stomach groans, loudly, too loudly – *Damn I'm hungry!* Making love all day will do that to a person.

Tristan starts chuckling behind me.

"Oh no!" I turn my head and kiss him. "I'm sorry I woke you."

"Don't be," he smiles so sweetly at me and kisses the tip of my nose.

"But you looked so peaceful and happy," I reply.

"I'm always happy when I'm with you, be it in my waking or sleeping hours," he replies, kissing my lips again.

"You say the sweetest things baby," I kiss him again, and gaze up at my husband, completely and utterly in love with him.

"You're hungry," he states and goes to move.

"No, wait!" I plead. "Stay here, just a few more minutes," I add and close my eyes again.

"Er...Coral," Tristan whispers.

"Mmm?" Is all I can reply.

"I need to pee," he chuckles.

Oh well, I guess the wrapped up in each other's arms is over for now. "Ok," I smile widely at my man and release his arms.

He bounds out of bed as though he's had a full night's sleep – which he hasn't – and I watch, with the biggest grin on my face as he saunters his sexy, naked body into the en-suite. *Damn, he has a cute ass!*

"Mmm..." I reach my arms up and have a good stretch, my muscles protesting slightly, but feeling glad that I cancelled mine and Tristan's training today with Will.

He is now Tristan's personal trainer too. And I no longer go to the gym. Will comes here for both Tristan and me, and we train downstairs, in the gym. I look up at the ceiling reflecting again on how much has changed this past couple of months. At the recommendation of my physiotherapist Raj, who I am still seeing as my shoulder still needs work after being shot by Susannah, Tristan hired a personal yoga teacher for me. Sam is amazing, and she has helped me become more flexible than I have ever been.

Yoga really helps with those certain...let's say...positions one finds themselves in when getting down and dirty with their man. I can't help chuckling at that thought, Tristan and I really go to town sometimes, but I'm presuming it's like that for every couple that is in a safe, intimate and very loving relationship.

I stretch again, feeling my shoulder twinge a little, and slowly sit up.

Tristan comes out of the en-suite, with dishevelled sexy hair, and smiles his most sexy smile at me. I watch as he pulls his grey baggy PJ bottoms on, commando style, and pulls on a white vest, making me swoon at him – He really does have the most gorgeous shoulders, strong and wide, and very sexy.

I smile coyly at him. "What's your hurry?" I question, and pull back the quilt so he can climb back into bed with me.

His grin widens as he crawls up the bed towards me. "Out of bed woman, you need to eat." He states, with a quick, chaste kiss on my lips, and a sexy slap on my ass, which makes me giggle. "Come on," he orders.

"Yes sir," I salute him, making him smile again.

He stands and walks towards the bedroom door. "If you are not downstairs in five minutes you are going to be in trouble young lady!" With that, he opens the bedroom door and saunters out.

FIVE MINUTES LATER I am sat on a breakfast stool, watching Tristan whip up some scrambled eggs for us. He has coffee brewing and bread toasting. It smells divine. My stomach grumbles in appreciation. The radio is playing Christmas songs in the background, and right now Greg Lake is singing 'I Believe In Father Christmas' – One of my favourites, so I sing along, much to Tristan's amusement.

And as I do, I can't help thinking back to us all decorating the house. It's a big house and took a lot longer than I remember it taking with Gladys. Which makes me think of my studio, and the tiny Christmas Tree I used to have, it was the only Christmas decoration I used to put up. I wonder what happened to it? – And for some reason, I'm consumed and overwhelmed again by the moment.

Tears spring to my eyes as I think about all that has changed. I no longer live at my studio, dreading and counting down the days to Christmas, knowing I was going to have to put on a brave face for so many days as I stayed over at Gladys'. I never have to do that again. I'm no longer a lonely singleton, and I never have to spend another Christmas wishing the right man would come along and whisk me away on a sleigh. I blink back the tears as I gaze at the mini Christmas Tree sat on the breakfast bar – I think we went a little overboard with the decorations, but hey, it's Christmas!

The house, however, seems eerily quiet with only me and Tristan rattling around in it. Danny is staying at Joe's until next week, as his news was good, a big old yes from Joe, so I felt it was needed, not that I've told Tristan yet. Although Danny's not sure what's happening over Christmas, something about Joe's parents coming to hers this year, so he'll probably stay with them. I am resigned that it will be another no.

It feels strange without Edith here though, I guess I've finally got used to having her around, I've been very thankful for her actually. Working full time at my new venture, the sandwich shop Tristan bought for me has been hard work. All the re-fitting, decorating, new menus and systems, have made a huge change, and I've been so tired by the time I got home, that it's made me really appreciate Edith, having a meal ready and waiting has been wonderful – I'm a lucky girl, I know that.

Edith told me the day we were decorating that she's always gone away for Christmas, to her daughters, that she loves the build-up, and that it's even more special and magical since her granddaughter arrived. Edith said she just loves seeing the excitement on her face as it gets closer to the big day when Father Christmas comes down the chimney, which makes me think of Tristan and me, and the fact that he has me now.

The thought of him on his own last Christmas, in pain and grieving the loss of his folks, washes over me again, making me shudder slightly – but I refuse to let it take hold. So I take a deep breath, clear the feeling, and think of how lovely our day has been so far, and I'm soon back into the happy mood I was in a couple of minutes ago.

"Want some help?" I ask Tristan, but really I'm just enjoying watching him move around the kitchen.

"Nope, all under control," he replies with a sweet smile. "Besides, I wanted to cook for you."

"I like cooking for you too," I reply, and take a sip of orange juice.

"I know you do baby, and I love your cooking. But I wanted to treat my beautiful wife, who I haven't seen for two days, and who I have missed, to a late brunch."

My hearts swells with love. I blow him a kiss, which makes him smile widely. Then he saunters over with two plates and places them down in front of us. I have two pieces of thick granary toast that are piled high with scrambled eggs. *Oh not again!*

## A Christmas Wish

And I think once again, that I should take the opportunity to have that chat with him.

"Tristan, thank you, but I can't eat all that," I tell him. "One piece of toast and eggs is perfectly adequate!"

"Coral – You have lost weight again. Don't think I haven't noticed. You are far slimmer than when I met you, and it worries me. I want you healthy, not withering away in front of me." He's getting annoyed.

Not wanting another argument about it, I sigh and dig into my brunch. We eat silently for a few minutes, but I just can't help it, I have to say something. So I decide that now is most definitely the time for that chat.

"You know, I'm not going to keep telling you it's because I'm in love." I huff and eat another forkful of eggs.

"And I'm not going to keep telling you that it worries me," he replies, his fork mid-air, his look one of stubborn disapproval.

I narrow my eyes at him. "Ugh, you are so stubborn, you know that!"

"I could say the same for you," he replies and continues to demolish his food.

I look down at my plate, already feeling full and contemplate forcing more food down, but I decide against it. "I'm full," I tell him firmly, then stand and head over to the coffee pot.

When I turn around I see he's got his elbows on the breakfast bar, his hands are folded together and are pressed firmly against his lips. His chocolate brown eyes have turned to dark chocolate. He's tense. I can tell by the way the veins are sticking out in his forearms, and the darkness of his eyes. He does not look like a happy man. But I will not be dictated to. Certainly not on the amount of food I do or do not eat – *Jeez, I love him more than my life, but he really drives me crazy sometimes!*

"So what am I to do?" he asks; his eyes dark and foreboding.

"Get used to it," I tell him as I pour more coffee into our cups.

He sighs heavily. "Coral' – "No Tristan, don't Coral me. I am not starving myself. I love food. I don't have, and never have had, any kind of eating disorder. If I had, then I would totally understand your concern. But you are overreacting, and it's driving me crazy!"

He sighs again, unfolds his hands, and silently continues with his food. I add cream to our coffees, pick up my half eaten plate of food, feeling guilty that it's going to waste, and place it on the side. And then a thought enters my mind, making me freeze – *What if he's not as attracted to me as he was before? What if he doesn't find me as sexy as he used to?*

I swallow hard and turn to face him.

"Am I no longer attractive to you because I've lost weight?" I whisper, glancing down at the floor, I don't think I could take it if he didn't want me anymore.

"Coral, I think the fact that I couldn't wait to be with you when I came home last night and the fact that we have spent all day in bed. Plus the fact that no matter how many times I have you, I just want more, should prove to you that I'm crazy about you. I am a very happy man who is very much in love with his wife." He tells me in a very formal tone.

I can tell he's still not happy with me. Otherwise, he would have stood up, come over to me then taken me into his arms and eased my fears, which in a way he has done, I know that he is still attracted to me. And I start to smile at his words – *'I am a very happy man who is very much in love with his wife'* - Sliding back onto the bar stool, I pick up my coffee and take a sip, glancing at Tristan from the corner of my eye as I do.

"I'm sorry," I tell him.

With his plate cleared, he turns to me, wraps his arm around my waist, leans in and places a soft kiss on my neck. "Me too," he whispers.

"I'm in love with you too, but I do mean it, Tristan. This has got to stop. I'm ok." I tell him in a soft, pleading voice.

"Alright," he whispers, defeated.

"It makes me feel guilty," I tell him.

"Guilty?" He questions, sitting up straight, his brows pulled together in concern.

"Yes. I hate wasted food, you know that. So stop overfilling my plate. I know you're doing in out of concern, but I also know you're doing it in the hope that I will gobble it all up." I raise a sardonic eyebrow at him, which makes his lips twitch with a smile.

We stare at one another, for what feels like a long time, and eventually end up smiling, then grinning widely at one another. He takes my free hand and entwines it with his. I lean in and tenderly kiss his cheek.

"I'm right aren't I?" I question, even though I know I am.

He looks down at our hands and chuckles slightly, smiling that shy, cute smile that I remember from Munchies. The first day he took me to breakfast, the first time I heard him laugh, and I fall in love all over again.

"Yes," he chuckles, his answer hesitant, then suddenly he's my broody man again. His eyebrows are pinched together, as he stares down at our fingers. He looks up at me, all humour gone, reaches out and places his hand on my cheek. "My only concern is for you, for your health and your happiness."

"I know," I whisper back, and place my hand over his. "But does it really matter that much to you that I have lost a few pounds? You know I'm healthy, I drink enough vegetable and fruit juices to assure you of that, and as for being happy..." I stop, feeling too overwhelmed by the look in his eyes – *What is that?*

He takes a deep breath and hesitates for a moment. "And are you...happy, here now, with me?" he asks.

I sit up straight, feeling panicked that he is feeling unsure of himself, so it's my job to assure him in the strongest possible way, how I feel about him.

"Yes," I answer firmly. "All of the time, which is a world away from how I used to feel. Don't you understand Tristan? My life, this life I now have with you, is everything I ever wanted and needed. I am happy, all of the time. Even when we fight, or I wake from a bad dream, or I'm tired and cranky from a busy day in the shop...at my very core, my very centre, I am happy." I take a deep breath, hoping I've explained myself correctly and eased his fears.

"Just like me then," he replies, and smiles so warmly at me, it shakes my insides – *God I love this man!*

"Oh, and just so you know, I happen to like being this slim, I *feel* really good Tristan." I add, purposely emphasising the 'feel' part – because I do feel really good.

He raises an eyebrow at me, so I jump in again before he can say anything about that. "Promise me you won't pile loads of food on my plate again?"

He's deadly serious now. "I promise, faithfully, that I will never do it again." I feel the profound truth of his words, I can see it in his eyes, the intensity, the solemn promise made that will not be broken, and I feel like we are in the midst of our wedding vows.

"Thank you, baby, for understanding, and in return, I will try to...eat more...snacks...or something," I say as a goodwill gesture.

To this reply, he grins widely, then turns to his newspaper, picks up his coffee and begins reading. And I say a prayer that the whole 'eat more food' thing has passed, and he won't moan at me anymore. Picking up my coffee, I slide off the breakfast stool, head over to the sofa and curl up against the big pillows, wondering what we are going to do for the rest of the day...

I'M WOKEN FROM my snooze by Tristan getting to his feet, walking over to me, and then holding his hand out. I guess our very late night and extracurricular activities have caught up with me.

"Dance with me?" he asks. And I notice Nat King Cole is singing The Christmas Song, he's one of Tristan's favourite artists, and I have to agree, he has a wonderful voice.

I smile, feeling silly as we are both in our sweats and vests, but gladly take his hand. "Why thank you," I tease as he helps me to my feet - And I know that we should take this opportunity of just us in the house, although in saying that, Tristan is not shy about dancing with me in front of Danny or Edith.

He spins me once as we dance towards the windows, closer to the Christmas Tree. I giggle in delight as Tristan tips me back, my hair touching the floor, then brings me back up and kisses my cheek. *Oh, I love this. I love him.*

I lean closer, pressing the full length of my body against his so we are cheek to cheek, and on my tip-toes I softly sway with him, enjoying the song, the music, the moment. And feeling grateful that even though we do drive each other crazy sometimes, and we do fight, we also have the ability to say sorry and kiss and makeup, the argument forgotten; I love that neither of us holds grudges. I ponder that for a moment - *Maybe that's what makes us work so well together?*

As the song comes to an end, Tristan tips me back again, his eyes dancing with mirth. "Thank you for the dance wife," he says and pulls me back to a standing position, making me laugh as he does. And I'm suddenly struck again with the realisation of how different I feel, compared to how I used to feel. And how much happier I am on a day to day basis.

"What is it?" His hand is against my cheek, his humour gone. "I've seen that expression on your face maybe half a dozen times since we married. I've always wanted to know what it means," he adds.

I swallow hard and try not to get too overwhelmed as I attempt to get the words out. "Just...' I shake my head and take another breath. "It's just that...every now and then, I get this feeling..." I look up at him, feeling lost for a moment as I stare

## A Christmas Wish

into the depths of his big, beautiful brown eyes, his freckles, his dimples, his full soft lips – I'm swooning again at my husband.

"Go on baby," he softly prompts.

I blink a couple of times, trying to re-fire my brain. "Um...ok. So, I just get this feeling...that stops me in my tracks...because my life is so different now..." I look away, and frown at the floor, knowing I'm not getting this out right.

"Are you unhappy about something Coral?" His voice is tender.

I look up at him and shake my head.

"I have no need to worry?" He asks.

I shake my head again – *Tell him Coral!*

"The opposite," I whisper, he eyes are searching mine, trying to find the answer. "Tristan, when I think back to how I used...no, let me try it this way." I take another breath and begin blurting it out. "Every now and then, when I'm with you, I get this feeling, like a reminder of how unhappy I felt. I was trapped inside my own head, never moving forward. Afraid of everything and everyone, unable to really let anyone in, and love them completely, not even my own family, for fear of them leaving or rejecting me," I take another breathe and continue.

"It feels like it never happened now, that I didn't go through all those years of such deep unhappiness. I don't know why that is, and sometimes I get a little scared that this is all so surreal that I'll wake up one day, back where I was." I bite my bottom lip, hoping I explained that right.

"My life has changed so much, all because of you. I love...wholeheartedly now without fear or hesitation, and it's a wonderful feeling...it really is..." I say with a giggle-sob, my nose tingling as I try to hold back the tears.

"Oh, baby!" Tristan wraps his arms around me, squeezing me tight. I reciprocate and wrap my arms around his back, holding him tight. I close my eyes and listen to the sound of his heart beating, and rest my cheek against his strong chest. We stay like that for a while, and I melt against him, my sweet, loving man.

"Coral..." I look up at him, resting my chin on his chest. He smiles so sweetly at me, I feel my legs shake with the adoration I see swimming in his eyes. "I don't think it's just because of me," he whispers.

Always so modest - My sweet, sexy man.

"Yes, it is Tristan. You gave me the strength to believe that I could love, without getting hurt. You fixed my broken heart my darling, and for that, I will always be grateful." I close my eyes and rest my head against his chest again. I really love his hugs, and his kisses and his - "Baby, have you done any Christmas shopping yet?" Tristan asks, halting my thoughts.

"No," I chuckle, thinking how much I actually have to do.

"Shall we go out tomorrow?" He asks.

I look up at him. "You want to take me Christmas shopping?" I ask, feeling gleeful that he does.

"Yeah," he chuckles, 'unless you'd rather do it on your own?" He asks.

"No!" I say a little too eagerly, which makes him smile widely.

"Ok," he laughs, 'we'll get everyone's presents sorted tomorrow. And then you can relax about it," he says.

I frown up at him. "Why, do I look stressed?" I ask.

"A little," he replies and runs his forefinger underneath my eye.

"I'm ok," I tell him, and take his hand in mine. "I just... couldn't sleep without you next to me," I admit, wondering if it makes me sound like a loser who has no life without him.

"Me neither," he whispers back. "Which is why I want you to come with me next time," he says, serious now.

I look down at his chest, feeling guilty. "Is that because you came home to me having a nightmare?" I quietly ask, feeling guilty.

He tips my chin up, so I have to look at him. "No, it's not. I missed you. So I'm asking if you'll do me the honour of coming with me next time I have to travel."

I smile widely at him. "In that case, yes, I will," I say, knowing I'll probably feel a lot better about it too.

"Good." He says and lifts my hair from my shoulders, so it falls down my back, and then he leans down and kisses my exposed neck and shoulder, sending shivers all over my body.

"Tristan," I mewl, my eyes closing, my head falling back to his touch.

"Yes," he chuckles, his lips still planted on my skin.

"Take me to bed and then shower with me," I manage to whisper.

"With pleasure," he says – And the next thing I know he's swung me over his shoulder, making me scream in delight, and is running up the stairs, obviously eager to execute my plan...

# ELEVEN

*Tristan*

I LOOK DOWN AT CORAL, who's busy wrapping Lily's Christmas Gift on the floor by the fire as she watches National Lampoons Christmas Vacation - and I smile. Maybe it's because it's Christmas, or the fact that I no longer have my folks, maybe it's both those things combined, but as I look down at her, I feel very lucky and grateful that she's in my life. It warms my very soul. *Work Tristan!*

I manage to pull my gaze away, I'm supposed to be checking out the end of year revenues, but it's a damn hard task with Coral in the same room. *Concentrate Tristan!*

Coral bursts out laughing at something that's been said in the movie, and I look down at her again, completely captured. She looks like a fucking angel in her new cream jumper dress that I bought for her, her dark shiny hair is curled and flowing down her back, and her makeup is soft, making her look fucking edible.

I sigh, knowing I'm going to have to go into my office if I'm to get any work done, but also not wanting to leave her side, she really is something. I see it all the time when we're out and about - Men looking at her. It takes all of my willpower not to have words with some of them, as they are so blatantly staring at my wife, and I can see how uncomfortable it makes her, but it kind of comes with the package. A blindingly gorgeous face like Coral's will always bring unwanted attention, add in the killer body, and she's every man's fantasy.

I quickly scratch that thought – I don't want any fucker thinking of my wife that way.

My mobile vibrates. I place the paperwork on the coffee table, grab my mobile and check it. An email from the flower company I ordered from last year. The Christmas wreaths I ordered are ready. I swallow hard, knowing this is going to be one hell of a difficult task, but one that I want to do – at least I'll have Coral by my side this year.

"Baby,' I look down at her, feeling a lump form in my throat, 'the wreaths are ready," I manage to say. Coral nods once, and then without a word she gets to her feet, sits next to me, kisses my cheek and wraps her arm around my back.

"Ok babes,' she whispers softly, 'you say when you want to go." With another kiss on my cheek, she lays her head on my shoulder and closes her eyes.

I swallow hard again. "Tomorrow, I want to do it tomorrow. Danny can drive us there and back. We'll leave early, miss the traffic. I just want it done baby." I feel my cheeks flame as I think about it.

"Ok, whatever you want," Coral reaches her hand up, places it on my cheek, and turns my face towards her. Her lips reach mine, and tenderly she kisses me, making my eyes fucking water with how sweet she is. *Christ!*

I pull back, kiss her forehead and stand. "I've got work to do. I really need to finish as we won't be here tomorrow." As I lean down to pick up the paperwork, her hand stops me.

"Tristan," she softly says and entwines her hand in mine. "You don't need to do that right now."

And I know she's right. I nod my reply.

"Come here baby, come lie down with me," she softly adds.

She cradles me in her arms, my head on her chest, and she's running her fingers through my hair, her other hand is gently stroking my back – and I feel like a child again. "I love you Coral," I breathe out, feeling grateful for this.

"It's going to be a tough day," she whispers, kissing the top of my head.

"Yeah..." I breathe and hold her tighter to me.

"Did you want to stay over at a hotel?" she softly asks.

"No. I want to come home baby," I quietly reply.

"Ok babes, whatever you want." She kisses the top of my head again, and I feel wrapped up in her warmth. We stay like that for a while, and I bask in the feeling, knowing no other woman could make me feel this way, so loved and comforted in my moment of grief.

"Are the wreaths being delivered here?" she softly asks.

"Yeah...all three of them," I reply. For Granny & Gramps, one for Coral's mother, and one for Susannah. I still can't get my head around the fact that Coral wants to lay one against her grave – she's too compassionate sometimes, but then again, I wouldn't change her for the world.

"I thought we could go and see Granny & Gramps first, then head over to your mother's grave. Get it all done in one day. We can eat out for dinner if you want to?" I suggest.

"Why don't we wait to see how you feel when we get back, you might not feel like going out," she softly says, her hands still running rhythmically through my hair – it's making me feel very sleepy.

"Ok," I murmur, my eyes feeling heavier and heavier as I drift away, safe in my baby's arms...

THE FOLLOWING DAY, we arrive at the cemetery. I'm trying to hold it together, for Coral's sake. I hate being upset in front of her, but I cannot clear the lump in my throat. Opening the boot, I pick out the wreath for Granny & Gramps and close the boot back up.

Coral is there, at my side. She entwines her hand in mine and looks up at me with sad eyes. I almost lose it. Instead, I take a deep breath, squeeze her hand, and we start walking towards their graves. The day is incredibly cold and foggy, making it hard for me to find my way to them, but eventually, I do.

"It's here," I whisper to Coral, and stop in front of the headstone.

"My forever love," Coral whispers, reading part of the engraving out loud.

I swallow hard against the lump. "It's what Gramps always called her," I manage to say.

"That's sweet Tristan," she rests her head against my shoulder and gives my hand a squeeze. They are buried together Granny & Gramps, in the same plot, as they always wanted. They also wrote their own words that they wanted on their headstones. I want to read it aloud, lay the wreath down, wish them a Merry Christmas, and say my goodbyes, but I cannot seem to find my voice.

"Coral will you..." I nod to the headstone.

"You want me to read it out loud baby?" she softly asks.

I nod my reply.

"Ok," she says, her voice is sweet and angelic. Then she takes a deep breath, pulls her shoulders back, and begins. "Here lies Frederick Freeman. Devoted and loving husband to his forever love Rose Freeman. She lies here also, by her husband's side, together for eternity. You will always be in my heart, your Son – Tristan." Coral reaches up and silently wipes away her tears with her hand. "You want me to read the poem baby?" she croaks.

I nod my head again, and swallow several times, trying my best to keep it together.

My brave girl takes a deep breath and begins reading.

"And so our time has come my love, we have perished and are now above. United once again I see, so very much we are meant to be. In life, I loved you heart and soul, so blessed to have been given that role. To our darling Tristan who we have left behind, we pray you find a love as divine. God bless you, child, may you be safe. You brought us such joy throughout our days. Spread your wings and open your heart, she will find you one day, and will never part." Coral looks up at me, tears bouncing down her cheeks. "Tristan, that's so beautiful," she whispers.

I crumble, knowing their wish has come true, and cry like a fucking baby. I did find that girl, Coral is here, and they'll never get to meet her. I squat down in front of their grave and really let go. I feel Coral crouch down next to me, and placing her arm around my back, she brings me the comfort that I need.

Silently she waits until I am done.

I look down at their grave and place the wreath in the centre of the headstone. "Miss you," I manage to say. I take a breath and attempt to compose myself. "Merry Christmas Gramps, Merry Christmas Granny. I love you." Tears are streaming down my face. I don't understand why I'm crying so much.

"Merry Christmas Granny & Gramps," Coral whispers, I glance at her and see she's crying too. "I wish we could have met, but I'm sure we will one day." She blows them a kiss, breaking my fucking heart with how sweet it was to do that.

I stand, Coral follows my action, and we wrap our arms tightly around one another. And I feel comforted and blessed to have such an amazing, sweet-natured woman by my side. I don't think I'd have done this if I didn't have Coral here with me. I gaze at the headstone for a few more minutes, saying my silent goodbyes, and when I'm done, I look down at Coral.

"Are you ready to go?" I ask.

"Whenever you are baby," she softly answers.

"I'm ready," I say.

"Ok," she whispers, and we walk arm in arm back towards the car...

## A Christmas Wish

ARRIVING BACK IN Brighton, I have to wake Coral to let her know we have reached the cemetery. The weather is still as bad, if not worse, the sky darkening, the temperature dropping rapidly. I want to get Coral back to the house, I'm worried she'll get cold standing out in this weather.

"Ok, let's do this," she says and exits the car.

I quickly follow and grabbing the two wreaths, we head over to her mother's grave. "I'm not going to do this every year Tristan, but felt like I should this year." Her voice is almost a whisper, and she's frowning.

"I understand," I tell her, squeezing her hand.

She suddenly stops and looks up at me with wide eyes. "I didn't mean that the way it came out Tristan, I'm so sorry."

"It's ok baby like I said, I understand' – "No it didn't...' she sighs, then looks up at me again, "What I meant to say was I don't want to come here, to my mother's grave. That doesn't mean I don't want to see your folks every year, I should have said that." she adds, and I can tell she's castigating herself.

"Hey," I place my hands on her cheeks. "I know what you meant darling," I tell her, and force a smile, but I can't shake the sadness that I'm feeling today.

She shakes her head at herself. "Good job you know me so well," she replies.

I lean in and kiss her, then take her hand and we're on our way again. Reaching her mother's plot, Coral takes the wreath, kneels down and lays it against the tree.

"Hey mom, hope you're ok, wherever you are. I thought I would come and say hello, and bring you this. It's Christmastime you see... so Merry Christmas." She pauses for a moment, her eyes closed. "Love you, mom. Miss you." Coral stands and takes my hand again.

There are no tears, but I can tell she's deep in thought, no doubt thinking about the past, and all the awful things her mother did, and all the things she didn't do. It makes my blood boil, but I can't show it, I don't want to upset her.

After a few moments, she turns and looks up at me. "Susannah's?" she asks, and I hand her the wreath.

Coral places it down on her tree. "I hope you have found them, your baby and your husband, and that you are happy now and at peace. God bless Susannah and Merry Christmas," she whispers.

I pull Coral into my arms again. "Thank you, baby," I whisper.

Today had to be done. I wouldn't have felt right if I hadn't gone to their graves, like I did last year, and wished them Merry Christmas. Sounds silly, I know, saying those words to a grave, it's not like they can say it back, but as a sign of respect, and for the love they gave me, it's not only my duty but my privilege too.

Coral squeezes me tightly. "Let's go home baby."

I couldn't agree more. Taking her hand, we head back towards the car and the comfort of our home together...

# TWELVE

BACK AT THE HOUSE, we silently make our way down the hallway and reaching the sofa, Tristan flops down onto it, totally dejected, and stares out of the window. I've never seen him like this before, but I know I must be strong for him, so I turn on the Christmas Lights and the fire, say goodbye to Danny who's staying at Joe's, then I walk back over to Tristan and kneel down in front of him.

"What do you need baby?" I softly ask with my hands on his knees as I try to comfort him. This was such a hard day, but so much harder for him, than for me. He looks down at me and softly shakes his head. And my heart breaks for him.

"Oh baby," I whisper, and rest my head on his knee, trying to bring him solace.

"I'll be alright in a while," he croaks.

I look up at him again. "Did you want something to drink or eat?"

He frowns deeply as he considers this. "Yeah...a Brandy and a cigar," he says.

"Coming right up," I softly tell him.

He nods once at me, and I want to burst into tears, so I quickly turn away so he can't see my face because the look on *his* face is just heartbreaking. I wish I had the power to turn back time so we could have his folks here with us, just for a day.

"Thank you Coral," he breathes as I get to my feet, I turn back and manage to smile then silently walk down the hallway.

As I head into his office, I'm reminded of the surprise on his face when he opened this particular present for his birthday. Which I was really glad I had purchased, because the trip to Spain for Tristan's birthday, the one where I'd bought him flying lessons, had to be cancelled after what happened with Kane – we plan to take that trip sometime next year.

At the safe, I punch in the code and open the door. Picking up the heavy leather box, which is surrounded by layers of orange velvet, I carefully place it on Tristan's desk, open it up, and take out one of the cigars, which are individually packaged in frosted tubes.

This particular brand is a limited edition, and I had no idea when I bought them if he would even like them. But the Black Dragon Tubo is apparently one of Ghurka's rarest and most unique ultra premium cigars. And although I didn't understand all the lingo they use, as in what type of leaf is used and what kind of fillers, I thought they must be good considering how much they cost – a whopping one hundred and fifteen thousand pounds for a box of twenty.

I did a lot of research to find these for Tristan. And I'm so glad I did as he said it was one of the best presents he has ever had, and that the cigars are the best he's ever smoked, along with the ridiculously expensive Brandy that I bought to go with them, which apparently to the cigar connoisseur, is a must.

Placing the cigars back in the safe, I carefully pick up the large gun metal grey leather box that houses the very unique and ridiculously expensive bottle of Cognac inside it. Remy Martin's Louis X111 Cognac, Black Pearl Anniversary Edition, is the 4th most expensive liquor in the world. And when I came across it, I knew I just had to get it for Tristan, as he does love his Brandy. But my hopes were soon dashed when I found that only seven hundred and seventy-five decanters were made, hence them being a limited edition, and I didn't think I would be able to get one for him.

But after hours and hours of searching, I found this wine merchant in London, who managed to locate one for me, including the box for twenty-nine thousand pounds. Which is a small sum, when you compare how much the cigars were, and why both the cigars and the Cognac are housed in this safe?

Placing the Cognac on his desk, I close the safe and punch in the code to lock it. Then I pick up the Cognac, the cigar, his cigar cutter, lighter and the ashtray from his desk and head back into the living room, only to find Tristan has disappeared.

Placing the items on the coffee table, I go in search of him but stop as I hear his footsteps coming down the stairs. Making an about turn, I walk into the kitchen and reach up onto my tip-toes to get a Brandy glass for him, and a wine glass for me, but I'm struggling – and once again I think about getting these god damn glasses moved. And he's by my side, his hand on the

## A Christmas Wish

small of my back, as he reaches up and collects two Brandy glasses.

"No Tristan," I say, trying to stop him. "I bought that for you, to enjoy with your cigars." I softly say.

"I want you to have one with me." He says, and so I nod once, not wanting to cause him any further pain by arguing with him.

With the glasses in his left hand, he silently holds his right hand out to me, so I place my hand in his, and we walk over to the sofa, noticing as we do, that's Tristan's changed from his suit into his sweats and a t-shirt.

As we sit side by side on the sofa, I watch as Tristan opens the leather box housing the Cognac, and carefully lifts the metallic decanter from the box. It's normally a see-through crystal, but the Black Pearl version of the original metal flask is made by treating the crystal using a unique plating technique, giving it a beautiful reflective quality. With myriad subtle contrasts of light and dark dancing across its surface, which they achieved by layering successive thin coatings of titanium, carbon and gold one upon the other.

It is said to be a true work of art. And I have to admit, it is beautiful, which I never thought I would ever say about a bottle of booze.

Tristan then pours the Cognac into the Brandy glasses, cut's his cigar, and hands one of the glasses to me. I take a sip, and it's like no other Cognac I have ever tasted. And I try to work it out in my head how much each sip must cost, but quickly decide against it, as I could be here all night.

Tristan then lights his cigar, taking several puffs as he does, and I inhale the smoke, loving the way it smells, which is so different to cigarettes, and lean back against the sofa, waiting for him.

Picking up his glass with the same hand he has his cigar in, he leans back against the sofa, places his ashtray next to him, and props his feet up on the coffee table. And then he takes hold of my legs and places them over his, so I'm sideways to him and places his arm protectively over them.

Taking a sip of his drink, he slowly swallows it, then he then takes another puff on his cigar, and I lean up a little and inhale again, which makes him smile.

"Did you want to try it?" He asks.

I shake my head, knowing I'll probably cough and choke, which I don't want to do right now.

"I don't mind," he says, a slight smile on his face.

"I'm good," I softly say, and take another sip of the Cognac, and let it sit in my mouth, warming me, and then I swallow, and it smoothly coats my throat. And as it works its way down, I notice there's no burning effect at all – it's so damn smooth – and I suddenly realise why it's so expensive.

I lean against Tristan, basking in his warmth, the only sound is the howling of the rain and the wind against the windows. And I wonder if I should put some music on then decide against it, as I think this is what Tristan needs, some quiet time to think.

"I'm sorry I'm being quiet Coral," he says.

"Don't be," I softly tell him, and gently squeeze his arm. "It's been a tough day," I whisper.

He nods his head, and takes another puff, and drink.

"Can I ask you something?" I whisper.

"You can ask me anything Coral," he replies, still staring out of the window. And I debate on whether or not it's a good time to ask and decide against it.

"Coral?" he prompts.

"Another time," I whisper.

He turns his head and looks down at me, his big brown eyes soft and full of love. "You've got a question burning inside you," he says, reading me easily, 'you have had since we left the cemetery, and I would really like you to say what it is," he adds.

I sigh heavily, frowning deeply at the glass in my hand.

"It's alright baby," he tells me, and softly runs his hands up and down my legs.

"Ok," I whisper, and take a deep breath. "You...you never told me, and I've never asked because I didn't want to remind you of it. I know it still hurts you so much to think about them being gone..." I stop, not really sure if this should be done now.

Tristan takes another puff and slowly blows it out. "You want to know what happened to them?" he surmises, and he's right.

I silently nod my head. It's very morbid, I know that, but I also want to know my man. I want to know everything he's been through like he does with me. And I know we are newly married, and really, we haven't known each other that long, but my life is his life, his pain is my pain – I want to share everything with him.

Tristan takes another sip of Cognac, and I wait until he's ready. "Gramps got sick...he had flu. We admitted him to the hospital, and after three weeks he came home, but he fell ill

A Christmas Wish

again not shortly after, I guess his immunity took a beating..." he stops for a moment and takes another puff and sip. "We did everything we could to help him recover, vitamins, minerals... whatever would help him back on his feet. But I came back from the office one day, I'd had a meeting I had to go to, and the ambulance was there taking him away." He swallows hard and stares down at the fire. "This time it was pneumonia, and he didn't recover." Tristan's takes a large sip of Brandy, and I notice his cheeks have flushed, and his eyes have darkened.

Tears spring to my eyes. "Oh Tristan," I croak, and lay my head on his shoulder. "That's so sad," I add, trying not to be tearful – I must be strong for him.

"Yeah..." he croaks, sniffing back the tears, and then I feel him plant a kiss on my head. "But at least he didn't suffer. I made sure of that, he was pretty doped up throughout his last days. But I was... besides myself, I didn't know what to do or say, especially to Granny. I could see it in her eyes you know, that she knew this was it, and there was nothing I could do to help her," he says, choking up again as he remembers.

"I'm so sorry Tristan," I softly say.

"I know you are baby," he croaks back.

We sit silently for a while, both deep in thought. And as we both take the last sip of Cognac, Tristan turns to me. "Would you like another?" he asks.

"No, I'm good thank you," I reply, so he takes my glass, places it on the coffee table next to his, along with his half-smoked cigar. Then he leans back, wrapping his arm around my shoulder as he does, and I cuddle closer to him by placing my arm around his waist.

"I'm not sure which was worse," he softly says with another kiss on my head.

And I'm afraid to ask, so I say nothing, not sure of what I should ask.

"I'm making you uncomfortable," he says.

"No," I croak, 'I just didn't know what to say to that," I whisper.

Tristan chuckles slightly. "Silenced," he mocks.

"Hey!" I protest lightly and then decide I will ask. "So what *did* you mean?" I add.

I feel him tense beneath me then sigh heavily. "Granny died in her sleep," he softly says, 'which in a way was worse than Gramps," he adds croakily.

125

I frown deeply at his words. "Why?" I whisper, thinking that would surely be the nicer way to go.

And I can tell he's trying not to cry. "I never got...to say goodbye," he chokes out.

I squeeze my eyes shut - How awful that must have been for him.

"Edith had gone out for groceries, so I decided to wake Granny, and I...I found her, lying there with a slight smile on her face...I thought she was dreaming. You remember me telling you that she whispered Gramps name before she died?" He asks. I nod my reply. "Well, that was earlier that day, I thought she'd fallen asleep...but later...when I touched her to wake her, she was cold," he says, and squeezes me tight.

I reciprocate, squeezing him back. "Oh, Tristan...I understand what you meant now," I softly say.

"I'm so lucky to have you," he croaks, sniffing again.

"Ditto baby," I croak back, trying hard to keep the tears at bay.

And then taking me by surprise, he gets to his feet, walks over to the fire and turns to face me with his hand in his pockets.

"I have something I want to tell you," he says.

And I know in that instant it's important – but I also recognise that the old me would have panicked hearing him say that, all kinds of crazy thoughts would have raced through my head in that split second, and I would have been defensive – yet, my mind is calm and quiet. I think I have finally got to the place where I'm no longer expecting the worst, and it's all because of the beautiful soul standing before me.

"Ok baby," I say, softly smiling at him.

He nods once then begins. "I want you to know that I didn't marry you out of loneliness. I didn't marry you because you just happened to be in the right place at the right time. I didn't marry you because you are so different to any other woman I have ever known. I didn't marry you because I could see us lasting like my folks. I didn't marry you because I wanted a family again, and I certainly didn't marry you because of your smoking hot body, and your desperately beautiful face," he smiles then, making his dimples deep, and the laughter lines around his eyes crinkle. And even though my heart has started pumping wildly against my chest, I manage to smile back at him.

He takes a deep breath then continues. "I married you because of the potential I could see, the potential I knew was there from the very moment we met, even though you tried so

## A Christmas Wish

hard to deny it, and that's why I pursued you. I had to know if I was right. You see, I knew that underneath that ten-foot wall you'd built around yourself that there was a young woman who was capable of very deep love. I could see underneath the pain, and the hurt, and the anger that there was a beautiful, compassionate, sentimental soul, with so much to give. I listened carefully when you talked about your family and friends, and I could see how fiercely you loved them, and how far you would go to protect them, you just didn't have a clue how to show it because you were so afraid of being rejected again."

Tristan stops for a moment, he's deep in thought, but I am stunned – totally and utterly stunned that he knew so much about me and that he felt that way. He could see straight through me and all my bullshit, and I'm so glad that he did.

He continues. "When Rob left without telling you why I could see the capacity you had to give of yourself and to help your friend. When Joe told you about her children being taken away from her, and you relayed it to me, I could see you have a lot of empathy for others. And when you told me of Gladys getting married, I could tell that beneath the fear of abandonment, you were so happy for her and that you'd hated the thought of her being on her own, and how relieved you were to know she longer had to go through that. And as for Bob, I could see how much you adored him, how much you loved him, which made me even more determined to keep pursuing you." Tristan walks over and kneels down in front of me, and I can feel the tears are about to start streaming down my cheeks.

"I knew,' he whispers, reaching up with his thumb to dash away a fallen tear. "That if I could somehow get you to open up to me, and give me one-tenth of the love you felt for Bob, your family and your friends, I'd be the happiest man alive." *Holy fuck!*

I am still sat on the sofa with a gobsmacked expression on my face, which I'm sure Tristan is finding amusing. And I realise this has got to be the longest speech he's ever made to me, bar his wedding vows.

"Tristan," I croak, my voice wobbling on me.

"There's more," he says with a sweet smile. "You make me a better version of me. You are strong and good and kind and compassionate, and so full of love, which is amazing considering what you've been through. I've met many people in my career that have had similar circumstances to you, and they've become these awful broken versions of the person they could have become, had those terrible things not happened to them. But they did, and never in a million years did I expect for you to say you have gone through what they had, and yet, here you are without any addictions. I don't think you realise how much courage and strength that shows my darling, and how much of a strong mind one must have to combat all of those things."

I shake my head, disagreeing with him but unable to say so.

Tristan smiles widely at me, takes my hands in his, and looks up at me with those puppy dog eyes of his. "I haven't told you this, but I get comments all the time when I'm at one of the offices, my employees have noticed that I am a very happy man, and when they ask me why, I say it's because of you. For the first time in my life, I actually feel complete, which is a really cheesy thing to say, I know,' he chuckles once to himself, 'but it's true. You're the first thing I think about when I wake, and the last thing I think about before I fall asleep, whether or not you are next to me. And when I'm away, I look forward to seeing you so much, and I miss you so much it fucking hurts. And when I'm with you, I just want to do everything within my power to make you smile at me the way you do, your secret smile that's just for me and no one else. And when we're together,' he says with a wink, and I know exactly what he means, 'you take me higher than I ever thought possible, you're everything to me, baby."

"Oh Tristan," I mewl, 'you're everything to me too," I whisper.

He takes a deep, satisfied breath. "Thank you, for today. I don't think I'd have gone through with it had it not been for you my love," he reaches up and places his hands on my cheeks.

"I'll always be here for you Tristan," I whisper back.

He smiles then, leans up and gently places his lips on mine...

TWO HOURS LATER, we are snuggled up on the sofa together. After feeling so moved by Tristan's speech, I made love to him, on the floor by the fire. I had to show him somehow how much I love and adore him, and I wanted to make him feel a little happier. Then we took a soak in the bath together, and while there we decided neither of us was in the mood to cook, so we ordered a pizza, and I suggested watching a Christmas movie together, a funny one, to lift his spirits, and that it was his choice.

Tristan chose Home Alone – a Christmas classic, which he'd seen once before, but it was years ago. And it has had the desired effect, as we have both laughed our way through it, and it has really cheered Tristan up, which has had a knock-on effect

## A Christmas Wish

on me. But as the credits roll, my mind starts to wander back to what George said to me, and whether or not I am secretly worried about being on my own with him over Christmas.

"Earth to Coral," he laughs.

I look up at him, feeling guilty I was not in the moment with him. "Sorry," I whisper.

"Talk to me baby," he says.

I sigh heavily. "It's stupid..." I mumble.

"Well, I can't agree or disagree on whether or not it is if you don't share it with me," he says, his one eyebrow cocked up. And I know he's right – *He's always right!*

"Fine!" I grumble.

"Hey," Tristan chuckles and gently pushes me back, so I'm lying on the sofa, and he's on top of me, his fingers running through my hair, his delectable lips inches from mine.

"Speak," he whispers against my lips, his lips twitching with a smile.

"Fine!" I say again, trying not to smile back at him.

His grin widens, knowing he has the desired effect.

"You really want to know?" I ask my eyes wide as panic sets in.

He frowns then and solemnly shakes his head once. "When are you going to learn," he whispers against my lips, and then gently kisses them, 'that you can tell me anything...anything at all, and it will never change how I feel about you," he says.

I sigh heavily. "Fine," I mumble, realising I'm saying a lot of fines.

Tristan chuckles and runs his finger across my bottom lip. "You know, normally, I'd be very frustrated by now that you're not sharing, but today, I couldn't be more relaxed," he says and kisses my lips again.

And I just blurt it out. "George thinks I'm subconsciously freaking out about being on my own with you over Christmas, and that's why I want to make a big deal out of it and have everyone over." There I said it.

And Tristan is laughing. "That's ridiculous!" He chortles. "I mean no disrespect to George, I admire the guy and am indebted to him for being there for you, but I don't think that's true baby," he says, with another kiss on my lips.

"You don't?" I croak, feeling unsure and emotional about it all.

"No, I don't," he says, as he stares down at me with those wide eyes of his.

I can't help frowning.

"Do you think you are?" he asks.

"I didn't think I was until George said that," I reply. "He said that I might be trying to deal with unconscious feelings," I add.

"And what are they?" he asks, kissing my lips once more. And I know he's doing it to help calm and assure me – and I fucking love the hell out of him for it.

I stare up at him. "Feelings of worth, of being enough, of... oh I don't know," I say, feeling as though I just want to forget about it. "I wish I hadn't said anything," I add.

"And you think I don't have some of those worries too?" he asks.

"You?" I choke out.

"Sure, why not? I've never spent Christmas alone with a partner before, so yeah...I have fears, and doubts, but maybe all couples do when they spend their first Christmas together," he says, his tone relaxed, and I know he's pondering out loud.

"Ok," I say, 'well...maybe I have been kind of worrying that you'll...get bored," I whisper.

This makes him chortle again. "You, my darling, are putting far too much pressure on yourself. I won't be bored, at all. The idea of relaxing, here in this house with you, from Christmas Eve all the way through to New Year's Day – Is like fucking heaven," he says and pecks my lips again.

"Heaven?" I whisper.

"Yeah...the best fucking heavenly Christmas ever," he adds, chortling again. "So please baby, just relax and try to put those worries out of your mind. You are worthy, you are enough, and I'm really looking forward to spending all that time with you. I can't wait!" he adds excitedly.

And I relax and smile up at him. "Ok," I laugh, as he looks like an excited kid again.

"Good," he says with another peck on my lips. "Now, did we finish the pizza?" he asks.

I can't help raising my eyebrows in amusement. "Seriously? You're hungry again?" I chuckle.

"Yes." He replies, laughing too.

"I told you we should have ordered the large!" I laugh, which I did. Three pizza slices are not enough to keep a man with an appetite like Tristan's at bay.

"Hmm..." he says, and suddenly bounces up from the sofa,

and pulls his mobile out of his pocket. "What flavour would you like?" he asks.

I can't help chuckling at him. "You're ordering another?" I ask.

"Yep!" he says, rubbing his hand across his taut stomach. "So, what would you like darling?" he prompts.

As I sit up, I suddenly realise I'm hungry too, but that probably has something to do with the fact that neither of us ate breakfast or lunch.

"Anything,' I reply, 'as long as it's not meat feast," I add, and head into the kitchen so I can get us two more beers. Noticing that my worries that were there in the back of my mind from my chat with George, are gone - And yet again, it's all because of the wonderful, hungry man that is my husband. Feeling buoyant about that worry being gone, I skip my way over to the fridge, collect two cold bottles of beer, and head back over to my man...

# THIRTEEN

THERE ARE ONLY five days to go until Christmas Day is here, and feeling relieved to be home, I shrug off my winter coat, hat and scarf, then hang them up in the utility room to dry off. As I return to the hallway and look down towards the living area, I realise how strange it feels coming home and not seeing Edith cooking something up in the kitchen, or Tristan downstairs waiting for me.

A slight shudder runs down my spine, as it reminds me of being in my studio, and I guess you could say I got used to being on my own. But now the thought of coming home and not hearing anyone saying hello, or how was your day, is quite frankly, terrifying - I quickly shake of that thought and start walking down the hallway. As always I have missed Tristan, and I'm looking forward to seeing him - *Hmm wonder where he is?*

Popping my house and car keys in my bag, I head over to the kitchen and dump my handbag on one of the breakfast stools. "Hey baby, I'm home," I shout out, as Tristan is clearly not downstairs.

I'm about to go and warm up by the fire, but my mobile vibrates, so I do an about turn, find it at the bottom of my bag and check it – A reminder to try calling Joyce again. I can't believe I keep missing her, at this rate I won't even be able to wish her a Merry Christmas, let alone invite her here!

I decide that after I've said hello to Tristan and warmed up, I'll try calling her. So with hands that are still cold, and hair that got a little wet as I headed from the car to the house, I scuttle as quickly as I can towards the fire that's blazing and begin warming my hands up.

I smile at how pretty the house looks. All the Christmas lights are on, making our little sanctuary look like a magical, winter wonderland. The Christmas Tree is reflecting off the fire that's burning, making the very large living area feel warm and cosy.

And Tristan has the stereo on, Nat King Cole is singing Unforgettable - It's a beautiful song. I close my eyes and allow his wonderful voice to soothe me for a moment, but the smell of cooking soon interrupts my mellow thoughts as it drifts over to me, I can smell Chicken...and garlic and something else that I can't put my finger on. *Brandy maybe?*

I smile widely, Tristan did say he would sort tea out as he's working from home today, which I guess he has – I'm so glad he's a modern man who's happy to share the chores – *There's none of that 1950's crap in this household!*

"Baby?" I hear him shout from upstairs.

"Yeah...I'm warming up by the fire," I shout back.

"You are not allowed up here, you understand?" He tells me in a voice that's not to be argued with. Curiosity gets the better of me, so I walk to the bottom of the stairs.

"Why?" I shout back all innocently, knowing full well I am winding him up.

I'm sure it has something to do with presents – And seriously, if it is more presents then he needs to stop – there are already so many piled up underneath the tree. In-fact, it's got so bad that I actually called Debs a week ago to warn her that if she drops by with Lily, she needs to give me enough notice so I can hide all her presents in the library. What with Lily still believing in Father Christmas, but thankfully that hasn't happened yet.

"Coral!" He shouts. "Don't you come up here!" He warns.

"But I'm cold. I want to get changed." I shout back as I try to stifle the laugh that wants to burst out of me. Thunderous footsteps come barrelling down the first flight of stairs – *Uh-oh!*

I quickly turn, giggling at the excited feeling, and begin to run, but Tristan is too quick for me. He's down the second flight of stairs before I can even make it halfway down the hallway, and has captured me around the waist, swinging me around to the sound of my laughter.

"You infuriating woman!" He scolds, but he's laughing too. "You weren't going to come up, were you?" He asks, wrapping his other arm around me.

"No!" I manage to say between the chuckles that are still escaping.

"You tease!" He chortles, and with my back to him and his arms wrapped around me warming me up, he leans down and kisses my cheek. "Are you still cold baby?" he asks.

"I was," I pant, still laughing a little, and turn to face him. "Hello," I smile coyly at him.

"Missed you," he replies.

"Have you now..." I tease back.

"Very much so," he replies. I smile widely, reach up and place my hands on his cheeks. "Christ Coral! Your hands are freezing!"

In the next breathe, I'm up into his arms, and he's marching over to the fire. He sits, cross-legged with me in his lap, places my hands in his, and blows hot air on them. Then rubs them, creating friction, which is helping them warm up quicker. *God, I love him for this, he makes me feel so cherished!*

"Why are your hands so cold?" he asks, in concern.

"Oh, I forgot to put my gloves on as I locked up the shop.' – "Where's Danny?" He interrupts; his tone suddenly serious.

"I dropped him off at Joe's," I reply.

"He didn't make sure you got home ok?" He asks; his tone sharp – He's not happy.

I sigh at his overprotective ways. "Tristan, there's only five days to go until Christmas. Joe's kids are excited, and he wants to be there to enjoy that. I can understand that, can't you?" I softly ask.

"He's supposed to be protecting you. That's his job and what I pay him to do," he replies sharply.

I frown up at him – *What's his problem?*

"Danny does protect me. He helped me lock up, we walked to the car-park together, and I drove him to Joe's, we were perfectly safe." I give Tristan a pointed look. I am not going to be happy if he starts arguing with me about Danny.

"Hmm, well as long as he did, and you're not just saying that." He asks with his eyebrows raised in disapproval. I can tell he thinks I'm covering for Danny, which is really annoying.

"Tristan, Danny would never forgive himself if something happened to me, or you. So no, I am not just saying that. Besides, I wouldn't want to lock the shop up in the dark on my own, especially when most of the offices have closed, it's kind of eerie down there at night - Danny knows I find it creepy."

Saying that throws me back in time to a few weeks ago, it was a Friday night, and Danny and I were locking up, but a stag party must have got lost and drifted into the commercial side of town. The moment I heard them I started to panic, but Danny was as cool as a cucumber. I can remember saying to him that we should run, but he told me not to worry and to finish off locking up, which I did.

At that moment, he really reminded me of Vinnie Jones, and that film he was in where he was the mobster. An actual shiver ran down my spine, because Danny just had this look on his face that told me he would take each and every one of them out if he had to, and I had nothing to worry about.

And to be fair, as we passed them on our way to the car-park, one of them made a comment towards me, and Danny just glared at him. Suffice to say we didn't have any problems, and all was well. But I don't want to tell Tristan that because the next thing I know I'll have three bodyguards.

I sigh heavily at the look on Tristan's face – he's still not happy.

"Look, I know you're a guy, and maybe guys don't really express that kind of thing to each other, but Danny does to me, and he cares deeply, about us both. Only this morning he was thanking us again for giving him a chance. He said that we have turned his life around by giving him this job."

Tristan doesn't look convinced. *Christ!* – I try to stay calm.

"Tristan, he is doing everything he is supposed to, if not more. I trust him, and I never trusted or felt comfortable with...' I hesitate a moment, and wince slightly when I say his name. '*Stuart*, so don't you go saying anything to him because if I lose him, I am not going to be happy – And before you say it, you can forget about me having anyone else!" I take my hands out of his and cross my arms.

He glares at me. "Are you done?"

"Yes." I glare back at him.

"Right, well what I *was* going to say is that we should get Danny a car," he says, his one eyebrow raised. I instantly feel guilty for going off at the deep end – *I'm still learning to be calmer, more patient.*

Tristan continues. "I want him to make sure you are safe from door to door. And no, I don't care who drives. But once he's got you home, he can use his own damn car to get to Joe's. That way, I'm happy, you're happy, and he's happy." He gives me a scornful look. "I had no idea you were so fond of him," he adds.

And I know what I've said has hit a nerve. "Don't say it like that Tristan," I mumble.

"Like what?" he asks, 'you were just gushing with joy about

your driver. How do you think that makes me feel?" he asks, then stands, not waiting for my reply, and walks away from me.

I debate for a moment on whether or not to follow him and decide I will. Getting to my feet, I stomp into the kitchen after him. At the slow cooker, Tristan lifts the lid and the most wonderful smell wafts towards me, making me lose concentration for a moment – *Coral, talk to him!* Right, yes – He doesn't know yet, and he should.

"Danny has proposed to Joe, and she said yes," I tell him, ignoring the fact that he's obviously got it into his head that I have some sort of feelings for Danny other than brotherly love.

Tristan silently puts the lid back on the slow cooker, crosses his arms and turns to face me.

I stare back at him. "Are you uncomfortable with Danny being my driver?" I ask

"You seem to have developed a close relationship," he replies, frowning back at me.

My heart sinks. "Tristan," I whisper and walk over to him. "Danny is like a brother to me. And yes, I do have feelings for him, but its brotherly love, that's all. And it's the same for him you know, he considers you, me and Edith his family," I softly tell him.

I know Tristan struggles with confidence and insecurity sometimes, as do I, so it's my job to comfort him and remind him of my love for him, but in this instance, it's Danny's life that will be affected by all of this – What if he can't get another job? What if he loses Joe? What if, god forbid, he goes downhill and ends up on the streets again, using drugs and alcohol? – The very thought of it is abhorrent - No, I cannot let that happen to him. Yet, Tristan and his feelings are my priority.

I sigh inwardly. "If you're uncomfortable with Danny being my driver…" I say, shaking my head at what I'm about to say, "then fine, I don't want you thinking something is going on when there isn't. So if you want me to have someone else, then we need to find him another job first," I add, feeling awful I just said that.

Tristan lowers his head and stares at the floor. His cheeks are starting to flame, and he's clenching his jaw – He's not happy about something. Then taking me by surprise he engulfs me in his arms, squeezing me tightly. "I'm sorry baby, I'm being stupid aren't I," he says, his voice all croaky and sexy.

"No, not stupid," I manage to say back, but it is hard to breathe.

A Christmas Wish

"Am I forgiven?" he croakily asks.

I pull back and look up at him. "There's nothing to forgive," I whisper back, then lean up and plant my lips on his for a kiss. "Are you worried about him being with me?" I ask, wondering if Danny has shown some sort of man sign that I haven't seen, but Tristan has.

He smiles his shy smile and rests his forehead against mine. "No...I just get a little insecure sometimes about you," he says with his eyes closed.

"Me?" I squeak in a high pitched tone.

This makes Tristan smile shyly again. "Yes, you," he says and lifts his head to look down at me. "You're so beautiful, inside and out. You're every man's fantasy," he whispers, frowning deeply at his own words.

"Hey," I say, and squeeze him around the waist. "You have nothing to fear Tristan. I will never leave you, or cheat on you... or do anything behind your back that could lead you to mistrust me."

He stares down at me, his eyes dark and intense. "I know,' he sighs, and places his hands on my cheeks. "I guess I get a little jealous sometimes when I see you talking to Danny. And I think it's because you two knew each other all those years ago, and I can't help sometimes wondering if...he's the better partner for you, because of what you both went through' – "Stop it!" I interrupt and take a breath.

"Tristan, there's no one else I will ever want but you," I whisper, feeling the sincerity of my own words.

This makes him smile. "Ok," he says, looking slightly relieved.

"Ok?" I question, smiling broadly at him, and he nods his head once. "So chef, what have you been cooking?" I ask lightly to ease the tension I can still see around his eyes.

His smile broadens. "We have creamy Chicken with veggies and herby dumplings, all swimming in thyme gravy. Did you want to try it baby?" he asks. *Sounds delicious!*

"Please," I say, my stomach grumbling, and I suddenly realise I didn't have any lunch. I will not be telling Tristan that though!

Tristan smiles at me, and lifting the lid he dips the spoon in, and carefully brings it back up, the gravy has steam oozing from it, I lean forward so I can taste it. "Careful baby, it's hot," he warns. And I just fall in love with him all over again – *He's so sweet!*

I blow a few times, then carefully take a sip of the gravy – *Absolutely delicious!*

"Well?" Tristan asks.

"Did you make this from scratch?" I ask.

"Yeah, I did," he proudly says. "With a recipe that Edith left for me," he quickly adds.

"Tristan, that's amazing! Well done babes," I say and give him a kiss on the cheek.

"It's good right?" He replies.

"Yeah, really good - I think we should use the slow cooker more often," I muse out loud.

He takes another sip of gravy. "You sure it doesn't need anything chef?" And I know he's teasing me.

I cock an eyebrow up at him. "No, it is perfect my darling, just like you."

He smiles widely at me and pops the lid back on. "It should only be about another half an hour," he softly says. "Would you like a glass of wine?" he adds.

"Please, but baby, do you mind if I leave you to it? I wanted to try Joyce again," I softly say.

Tristan bends down, so he's eye level with me – *I am such a short arse!*

"No baby, of course, I don't mind," he gives me a quick, chaste kiss. "I'll bring your wine over to you, ok?"

"Thank you, baby," I give him a kiss back, and with our moment about Danny over and done with, I skip towards the stairs so I can change from my work clothes, and try Joyce again...

ANOTHER DAY HAS passed. I am sat cross-legged on our bed with the landline handset in my hand, I'm about to try Joyce again as there was no answer yesterday. I'm starting to think it's all a bit odd really, not being able to get hold of her – I know Gladys spoke to her a few days ago because she told me. And now there are only four days left until Christmas Day, and I'm really panicking we won't get to say hello and wish each other a Merry Christmas.

I sigh inwardly and try to pick myself back up. Because although everyone has bailed on me bar Bob, I have to keep reminding myself of how lucky I am to have Tristan. And that I should appreciate the fact that rather than a big Christmas with family and friends, we're going to be having a very quiet and sexy Christmas – just the two of us, well, once Bob's back

## A Christmas Wish

at home. A delicious shiver runs down my spine, as I think of the very sexy Santa costume I have bought for Christmas Eve. I think Tristan's going to love it.

A smile spreads across my face as I think about the possibilities, his reaction, and the fun sexy time we're going to have. And then I get this weird sinking feeling, which I've had several times since this whole Christmas wish idea started, that Christmas just won't be right with it being just the two of us, that Christmas is all about family, and being with the ones you love – *Stop it Coral!*

I take a deep breath and shake away that thought, even though it keeps rearing its ugly head. *It's you and Tristan, stop being miserable about it!*

I nod my head at my own words and check the time again. It's 1pm here, so 8am in Florida, it should be a good time to call as Joyce has always been an early riser. And Tristan is downstairs training with Will, so hopefully, I won't be disturbed, and I can have a good old catch up with Joyce, that's if I can get hold of her.

I punch in the code, then the home number and wait to be connected. Then I think I may be disturbing them all having breakfast, I almost hang up, but it's quickly answered before I can do so.

"Hello?" I wait for the answer, hoping and praying it will be Joyce.

"Is that you Coral?" Jackie asks - Joyce's sister. Her English accent is still there, but it's now mixed with a slight Floridian accent. And my heart sinks.

"Hi Jackie," I reply, trying to smile.

"How are ya kid?" Jackie asks, sounding upbeat. She's always been just as lovely as Joyce. Jackie married Ben many years ago, they have two kids, who are grown and have their own families, so now they have eight grandchildren in total – they always have a big Thanksgiving together, but do their own thing at Christmas.

"Great thanks, and you?" I ask.

"Well, I'm fit to burstin', what with the amount of pumpkin pie I've been eating since we had the kids around for Halloween and Thanksgiving," she laughs.

"Sounds nice," I reply. "And your family, are they all well?" I ask.

"Fine and dandy thanks – you calling for Joyce?" she asks.

"Yeah...she around?" I squeeze my eyes shut, hoping the answer is yes.

"No honey, she's gone away for a few days," she tells me. My heart sinks even further, I'm gutted I've missed Joyce – again. But the last time I spoke to her, she didn't mention anything about going away.

"She's gone away?" I ask, already feeling worried.

"Yeah...she's um...she's gone to one of those spiritual retreat places," she tells me, but I can't help frowning at the way that she said it. And I've never known Joyce to be spiritual. *It's very odd.*

"Is she ok?" I ask Jackie. "I can come over, I want to see her." I quickly add, feels like a lifetime since we said our very teary goodbye.

Then I wonder if Tristan and I should use the tickets Joyce purchased for us on my birthday? A round trip to Florida over the holidays, it would put my mind at rest that she's coping with losing John. And then I remember we can't as we have Bob coming for Christmas Dinner.

"Oh honey, that's sweet 'n' all, but I think she just needed some rest and relaxation. It gets real crazy here in November with all the kids here. You want me to get her to call you when she's back?" she adds.

"I can't reach her on her mobile?" I squeak.

"No...she um...she didn't take it, they don't allow them at those places." Jackie sounds very odd, and as though she's making it all up – I wonder for a moment if Joyce is there, and she just doesn't want to speak to me.

"Oh...ok," I mumble, feeling the tears bubble up to the surface – *No, don't cry!*

"I'll get her to call ya honey! Gotta go, Ben's callin' me." Jackie hangs up, without even saying goodbye and I just sit there, staring at the handset, feeling totally and utterly dejected.

Tristan comes bounding into the bedroom, sweat bucketing off him, as he glugs down a big bottle of water. "Hello my sexy lady," he says, throwing his sexiest smile my way, and then a wink. He's obviously in a very jovial mood – I wish I were.

"Hey babes," I smile up at him, trying my hardest not to show him that I'm upset.

He waltzes over to me, leans down and plants his lips on mine. I can taste him and the slight saltiness of his sweat dripping down his face. "I'm going to take a shower. You can join me if you like," he winks at me again as he heads into the en-suite. *I must be a better actor than I thought!*

I smile back at him, but once he closes the door, I find myself drifting off, thinking about Joyce, remembering what it was like working for her, seeing her every day...and I want to cry, I'm missing her so much.

TRISTAN STARTLES ME by opening the en-suite door. He has a towel wrapped around his waist, his hair is all wet and sexy, and there are still beads of water dripping down his chest.

"Hey babes, shall we go out for something to eat? I thought it might be nice to visit North Laine and see the Christmas decorations. We could go ice-skating at the Royal Pavilion and visit the Christmas Market. Whatever you want to do, I just thought we've both been so busy, we should go out and have some fun. What do you think?" He asks, sounding full of the joys of Christmas.

"Sounds great," I reply, and it does, it really does. I'm just feeling a little melancholy, and I shouldn't be. I try to shake it off. I smile at Tristan as I watch him dress in a pair of dark denim jeans and a long sleeved t-shirt, which is a lovely mocha colour and hugs him in all the right places - But I guess there's no fooling my sexy hubby; he knows me far too well for that.

"Coral, why are you looking so down?" He asks. His eyes penetrating through me in the way that they do, it gets to me every time.

Getting to my feet, I turn away from him and place the handset back in the socket. "I'm not down," I answer, knowing full well that's not true.

"Yes." He sternly states and turns my body, so I have no choice but to face him. "You are," he adds.

I sigh inwardly. How do I tell him that the Christmas I so desperately wanted for him, for us, is still my Christmas wish, and that I'm really sad I haven't been able to speak to Joyce, without it sounding as though I don't appreciate the fact that I will have him all to myself?

"I just...wanted..." I stop, stuck for the right words to say.

"What my love, what did you want?" He asks; his frown deep.

"My first ever Christmas wish to come true," I whisper, feeling ashamed. "And I miss Joyce, I haven't been able to get hold of her again," I croakily add.

He smiles warmly at me, and softly strokes my cheek. "You have me now," he softly says.

I close my eyes in acknowledgement. "I know, and that makes me feel like the luckiest girl alive, but..." I shake my head, unable to say.

"But what?" He chuckles lightly. How he has this kind of patience with me, I will never know.

I sigh outwardly this time. "It's just...I wanted a big family Christmas, and even though I am resigned to the fact that it's not going to happen, I'm just...upset." Tears prick my eyes as I think of the Christmas I imagined, and the one that's going to be happening. And then I get a huge side order of guilt.

"Hey now...there's no need for tears." He says, and wraps his arms around me, pulling me closer to his lovely, strong chest. I surrender and wrap my arms around him, inhaling his scent as I do.

"Am I not enough?" He asks, and I can tell by his tone that he's being playful, but I also know that underneath that playfulness is an underlying tremor in the force, an insecurity that still plagues him. I will never understand why he thinks this way, and why he has these moments of doubt.

"You're more than enough Tristan," I tell him as I squeeze him tighter. Then propping my chin on his chest, I look up into his warm, chocolate eyes. "I just wanted *you* to have a big family Christmas," I add.

"Me?" He smiles warmly at me, his eyes swimming with love and affection.

"Yes, you," I tell him.

"I have all I need right here in my arms," he whispers sweetly.

"Oh Tristan...me too," I whisper back, and reaching up onto my tip-toes I kiss his lips. "And I know it sounds silly...but I wanted to make up for last year. You sat all alone on that beach on Christmas Day, without anyone. You'll never know how much it hurts me to think that you went through that alone. I just wanted to make this one extra special, that's all..." I close my eyes and rest my forehead against his.

"Oh, baby!" His arms squeeze tighter around me. And then I feel him kiss the tip of my nose. "It's very sweet of you to think of me that way darling. But I'm looking forward to this one because I have you to share it with."

I close my eyes again. "You're not sad...that' – "My folks won't be here?" he guesses. I nod, unable to reply. I don't want to upset him or have him thinking about the past, we had enough of that last week.

We both have to keep looking forward. Well, that's what George keeps telling me.

"Grief, my love, changes with time." He softly whispers. I

## A Christmas Wish

open my eyes and look up at him. "But it will always be there, I will always miss them. But the pain of missing them is not so hard now because I have you to hold me and to comfort me, beautiful you who makes my days so much brighter, and my nights so much warmer." He reaches up and places his hand on my cheeks, and just stares at me, in that way of his. How is it he always knows the right words to say? I feel that funny feeling in my abdomen again. Like my soul or my heart is expanding with love.

"So you're not sad we won't have a big Christmas?" I softly ask, searching his face for the answer.

He slowly shakes his head from side to side, keeping his eyes locked onto mine. I can't help swooning as I stare up at him. He really is the most beautiful soul I have ever known. I mean yes, he's handsome, really handsome, but there's so much more on the inside than I could have ever imagined.

"So, now that's out of the way. Would you like to go out and have some fun?" He asks.

He's definitely in high spirits, which really gives me the kick up the butt that I need. *Enough with all this melancholy Coral!* I will make it my mission to enjoy this Christmas with my husband, and not allow any sad thoughts to enter my mind. And to be fair, once I give myself a mission like this, I rarely fail - *Look out Brighton, the happiest girl in town is about to hit the streets!*

I can't help smiling at that last thought. "Yes, let's go and have some fun!" I say excitedly to Tristan.

"Ok baby," he replies, laughing at my expression. "Was there anything in particular that you wanted to do first?" He adds.

"No. I want to do all of it!" I say, and start bouncing up and down with excitement.

It's amazing what can happen when you really put your mind to something...

# CHRISTMAS EVE

THE LAST FOUR days I have to admit, have been magical. Once I got my head around the fact that this Christmas was not going to be like any other, and that it was going to be all about Tristan and me, I really started to enjoy it. It has been very special having him all to myself, and although I wouldn't have said this four days ago, I am actually relieved I don't have all that preparing and cooking and more cooking and hosting to do, and making sure everybody is happy and having a good time. The only thing I have concentrated on is Tristan and his happiness, and it has felt really, really good.

And as far as Christmas Eve's go this has to be the best one I have ever had. My morning started with being woken up by my lovely husband with breakfast in bed. And because he's a big softie with a heart of gold, he really thought about it, and presented me with pancakes – *Yes, pancakes!*

The first time we had breakfast together was at my studio back in July. I had almost broken my nose playing on the bouncy castle with Lily, and it was Tristan that stayed over and nursed me that night. I clearly remember him leaving the following morning to get us some breakfast, and my worries that he wouldn't return, but he did – with pancakes.

So Tristan presenting them to me this morning was a sweet reminder of how far we've come, and the wonderful, magical memories we have made so far. As we ate Tristan's homemade pancakes, we talked about that first morning we spent together, and he gave me his version of events. I cringed several times when he told me of how defensive I was, and then he told me a story about his folks and a talk they had with him not long after he split with Olivia.

His Granny had told him that he would meet the right girl one day and that she would love and cherish him, and his

Gramps had told him to stop being so nice, and to only open his heart to the woman that felt the same way about him. And then he told me all about how I was that girl, and that his Granny was right, that we really did meet each other at the right moment in both of our lives. *So true!*

After breakfast, we made love then showered together and made love again and then we went downstairs and opened a couple of presents we had both decided to give each other on Christmas Eve. Then the afternoon fun started. I got dressed up in my sexy Santa suit, and I don't quite know how it happened because we were in the living area, but somewhere in between the sexy fucking and drinking champagne cocktails, we have ended upstairs, lying on our bed.

Tristan turns on his side. "I have an idea," he says, running his hand up the inside of my thigh.

I can't help laughing, wondering what sexual delights he has planned for us.

"I'm all ears," I chuckle.

He hesitates taking a deep breath, then begins. "Coral, I have had so much fun today, it's been the best Christmas Eve I have ever had, but there's something else I want," he tells me.

"Anything," I whisper, wanting to make this his best Christmas yet.

He leans down and plants a kiss on my outer thigh. "I know this might sound…silly, but I…" he pauses, shaking his head at himself.

"What is it, baby?" I ask, placing my hand on his cheek.

He kisses the inside of my palm and keeps my hand held tightly in his. "I want to take you dancing," he softly says.

"Dancing?" I squeak, which makes him laugh.

"Yes," he chuckles.

"You want to go clubbing?" I ask, shocked by what he's asking.

He shakes his head with that shy smile I fell in love with. "No, not clubbing. I just thought, even though it's just us, that we could make the most of it. I bought you a dress you see, and I have a tux. So I thought it would be nice to dress up, drink champagne, and spend the rest of the night here, dancing in each other's arms," he says, and plants another kiss on my thigh.

I stare up at him, thinking how romantic it would be to spend Christmas Eve in my husband's arms, and what a wonderful idea it is.

"Tristan,' I whisper, smiling up at him. "I think that's a wonderful idea," I say.

His face lights up. "Yeah?" he says, excited now.

"Of course," I say, chuckling at his expression. "I couldn't think of a better way to spend Christmas Eve," I reach up and softly kiss his lips.

"Right then," he says, getting to his feet. He marches over to his closet, opens the door and disappears.

Then I remember what he said. "You've bought me a dress?" I shout out.

"Yes," he says, marching out of the closet with a big white box that has a red ribbon tied around it. "For you my love," he says as he places it down on the bed next to me.

I quickly get to a seated position. "Thank you, Tristan," I say puckering my lips for a kiss. He smiles broadly, leans down and gently plants his lips on mine.

"You, my lovely wife, are most welcome," he softly says against my lips.

I beam back at him, feeling completely and utterly in love.

"Open it then," he chuckles excitedly.

And feeling excited too, I lean forward and pull on the soft, red satin bow, and feeling a strange fluttering in my stomach, I slowly lift the lid. Inside is a red dress, it's a beautiful shade, that looks sparkly and Christmasey, and I'm already in love with it. I carefully lift it out of the box and fan it out.

It's a halter neck in the most beautiful material that has a really soft mesh overlay that glitters and sparkles as you move it. The bodice is fitted, and then the dress falls right down past my knees, very 1940's, and very sexy. I can tell Tristan has bought this particular dress because it isn't showing loads of cleavage if anything it's doing the opposite and leaving plenty to the imagination.

Tears bubble to the surface as I gleefully hug it to me. "Tristan I love it," I tell him.

"There's more," he says, smiling widely. "Look," he gestures with his head to the box again.

With an excited smile I lean forward, and inside the main box, is a smaller box with another red bow around it that I hadn't even noticed. Tristan holds his hand out for my dress, so I pass it to him, and as he carefully hangs it up.

I pick up the box, noticing it's heavy and pull the tie. Carefully lifting the lid, I find the most beautiful pair of red, sparkly, platform heels I have ever seen in my life, they match

## A Christmas Wish

the dress perfectly. They are sexy and elegant and - my breath catches, suddenly realising what they remind me of.

"What is it?" Tristan asks, already at my side.

I swallow hard and turn to look at him, and I find my voice is already telling him the story without my say so. "When I was little...before everything went wrong, I had a favourite dress and a favourite pair of shoes," I smile and shake my head, 'like most little girls do I guess. The dress was white and fanned out prettily, with a red shiny red belt that wrapped all the way around, and I used to feel like a princess when I wore it," I laugh again, remembering feeling like that.

Tristan smiles sympathetically at me, takes my hand he's been holding and gently kisses my palm.

I look down at the shoes again. "And the shoes...they were my Wizard Of Oz shoes. Like these,' I lift up one of the shoes Tristan bought me, 'they were so similar in colour, and whenever I wore the dress, I wore the shiny, red shoes." I take a moment and then continue. "I used to believe that if I clicked them together, that I would disappear to a magical place like Dorothy," I laugh again at hearing myself say that, even though it's true, Tristan chuckles once.

"And then, when things got bad, I used to hide under my bed, put them on and click them together, over and over again. Hoping that one of the times they clicked I would be gone from that place, and taken to a place of magic and wonder and happiness," I shake my head, laughing again that I actually did do that.

"Oh baby," Tristan soothes, softly tucking my hair behind my ear.

I smile shyly at him then frown. "Oh...I'm sorry," I say, starting to feel like an idiot for saying that and bursting the bubble of this lovely, thoughtful gift he has brought me. "I spoiled it...Oh, Tristan...I'm so sorry, I shouldn't have' – His lips reach mine, softly silencing me, and my guilt is easily forgotten.

"You've not spoiled a thing," he says as he pulls back. "That was very sweet Coral, and I think, that before everything happened, you must have been such a happy, sweet little girl, and if I met you back then, I'd have adored you just as much as I do now." Tears bounce down my cheeks at his words. "Hey now," he says, gently enfolding me in his arms.

I squeeze him tight, and immediately feel lighter, and so grateful. "Thank you, Tristan, for everything. For you, for this house, for how safe and secure you make me feel. For this beautiful dress and shoes," I croak, half laughing now.

Tristan pulls back, takes one of the shoes in his hands and inspects it. "Well I think," he says, glancing up at me, 'that you have new Dorothy shoes. New Dorothy shoes to start all over again in."

I gasp and look down at the shoes. "I do don't I," I say, my voice high pitched and excited, and tearful all at the same time.

"Click away my darling, because whatever you wish for, I will make it come true," he says.

"Tristan," I mewl, feeling so moved by his words.

I slowly fall towards him, knowing full well he's going to catch me and sink into his lap. I look up at him, feeling nothing but love, a pure unconditional love. His arms tighten around me, as he leans down and plants his lips on mine. And I close my eyes, feeling the safety and comfort of his arms holding me tight.

"Are you game my love?" He asks, and I know he means the special evening he wants us to have.

I open my eyes and like an excited child, I nod my head several times. His eyes crinkle at the corners as he smiles back at me, and his dimples go into overdrive. He's happy, which makes me so happy too.

"I shall go and get ready," I tell him in a teasing tone.

"Ok," he laughs, and helps me to my feet...

AS I STAND BEFORE the mirror in our bedroom, admiring the dress, but most of all the shoes, I realise I actually do feel like a princess. I have styled my hair in a forties wave and pinned up the right side, and matched my makeup to the dress, which means I have red lipstick on. And I feel like I should be in an American Christmas commercial - Tristan knocks on the bedroom door, pulling me from my crazy thoughts. After giving me this beautiful gift, he left me to it and showered in the spare bathroom downstairs, giving me strict instructions not to leave the bedroom, as he has another surprise for me.

"Come in," I softly say.

Tristan opens the door, and I drag my gaze away from the woman dressed as a princess and turn to look at him – and I'm blown away. He looks amazing, so dashing and handsome in his tuxedo, and it looks like the very one he wore when we married. His hair is styled into place, and he smells amazing.

"Wow," I whisper shyly. I still wonder sometimes how it is that he came to being mine, all mine.

"Beautiful," he responds as he walks towards me, his eyes filled with love and adoration.

I hold my hand out to him, and as he reaches me he gently takes hold of it, but then turns me so that I'm facing the mirror again, and he's stood behind me, his arms wrapped around my waist. And yet again, I can't help glancing at his wedding ring sitting on his finger, knowing that it represents us.

"Coral, you look amazing," he softly says, and gently kisses my naked shoulder.

"I only look like this because I happen to have a thoughtful, caring husband who buys me wonderful gifts," I tease.

"Oh yeah?" He says, teasing me back. "Well we better be careful he doesn't find out about us," he whispers.

I chortle at him.

"Are you ready?" he asks.

"Yes," I smile back at him in the mirror, and my excitement reaches an all-time high as I try to work out what it is that he has planned or bought me.

"Good," he says, and with another kiss on my shoulder, he smiles widely and holds out his hand. I gently place my hand on his, and we begin walking carefully down the stairs, but as we reach the top of the last flight of stairs, Tristan stops and turns to me.

"Wait here a second?" he asks.

"Ok," I say smiling widely at him.

He then runs down the last part, and when he reaches the living room, he stops and checks something out, then looks up at me and nods once. "Come on baby," he says, his hand held out to me.

I carefully step down the last flight, holding onto the bannister as I don't want to go flying in these heels, and reaching him I place my hand in his.

Pulling me to him, so my back is to the living area, he whispers, "I really hope you like this surprise," then he gently turns me around.

"Merry Christmas!" A loud cheer echoes out.

How I don't faint with shock, I don't know as all of my family and friends are standing in the main hallway, and they are all dressed up in swanky suits and beautiful dresses.

My chin has most definitely hit the floor. *What the hell?*

Everyone is here. Gladys and Malcolm, Debs, Scott and

Lily, Rob, Carlos and Mei, George and Phil, Danny, Joe and her kids, and Bob. For a moment, I think I'm actually having some kind of hallucination, then I think I must be dreaming, so I discreetly pinch my arm – *No, I definitely felt that.*

And I'm frozen to the floor, my legs wobbling slightly, as they all stand there smiling and laughing at me, loud and lovely, and full of Christmas cheer. Tears bubble up and spill over my cheeks. I literally am speechless. Tristan wraps his arms around me from behind and squeezes me tight.

"Merry Christmas my love," he whispers in my ear.

My hands come up to my face, I'm trying to stop the tears, and I'm shaking my head in wonder at it all. "You did this?" I manage to croak.

"Yes," he laughs.

"And they were all in on it?" I ask.

"Yes, it took some convincing," he says. *Explains the declines!*

"Oh, Tristan!" I gush, turning and crushing myself to him. Reaching up I kiss his cheek, then his lips. "What's happened to our sexy night together?" I whisper.

"We'll have plenty of those in Hawaii," he whispers, 'this is Christmas Coral, it's a special time of year when we should all be together - don't you think?" he asks.

I frown up at him. "But you said you didn't want me hosting!" I retort.

"And I don't," he replies, 'but this isn't hosting."

"It isn't?" I ask, wondering what he means.

"Later, I'll explain everything later. Come on darling, everyone wants to say hello," he whispers, rubbing my back.

I gaze up at his big, warm chocolate eyes. "Thank you, Tristan. Merry Christmas," I kiss him several times on the lips, 'god I love you," I add.

"I know," he laughs, 'as I love you. Now go and say hello," he orders.

I turn around, take a big breath and scream, "Merry Christmas!" out loud. And run towards Rob who wouldn't you know is at the front of the crowd.

Within minutes I have hugged and kissed all the people I love, except for one that's missing – Joyce. Right at that moment, the doorbell rings. I glance to my right to see Rob is busying himself by handing out cocktails that look ready-made, and I wonder how Tristan did all of this without me knowing.

And then I watch as Tristan waltzes down the hallway and opens the front door with a wide smile on his face. And in steps...Joyce? I take a second look, thinking that I'm imagining her there smiling back at me from the front door, but it really is her. Joyce is stood in my living room, here in Brighton – and I haven't seen her in what feels like forever – and I just want to burst into tears.

"Joyce!" I scream out loud, feeling rooted to the floor.

"Coral!" she screams in equal delight, as Tristan relieves her of her bags.

"You're here!" I manage to say, still shaking my head in wonder at it all.

Joyce smiles widely at me and nods her head, then opens her arms out wide, and without a second thought, I run towards her.

"Oh, Joyce!" I gasp as we embrace each other, holding on so tightly.

"Oh my dear, dear girl," she whispers, squeezing tighter several times.

"Joyce," I whimper because I have no idea what else to say – I think I'm still in shock.

"Oh, that's nice!" Rob pipes up, "We all make an effort, but does she want to' – "Oh be quiet!" Gladys and Joyce both say as they titter away at Rob.

Then my brain fires up. "Joyce," I say, pulling back to look at her, but still keeping hold of her arms. "What are you doing here...I mean, it's amazing, I'm so happy you're here, but' – "Tristan," Joyce answers, smiling widely at me.

"Tristan?" I whisper back.

"Yes,' she laughs, 'He called me about a month ago, and we talked for quite a while. He asked how I would feel coming back for Christmas, and told me of his plan to surprise you." I gape at Joyce, then turn and try to find Tristan who's got lost in the crowd.

"You didn't have a clue did you?" Joyce says her smile still wide.

I shake my head at her. "No," I manage to whisper.

And I suddenly realise this is the reason I haven't been able to speak to her, and the reason for that very odd conversation with her sister.

"How long have you been here?" I ask.

"I flew in a few weeks ago. I've been staying with Gladys and Malcolm," she tells me.

"Wait, so the other day when I was at moms' – "I was there," she says, her eyes glistening over with fresh tears.

"Oh, Joyce!" I cry, and we embrace each other again...

I HAVE NO IDEA how much time has passed, but it's pitch black outside, making the house feel warm and cosy, and so Christmasy now that everyone is here. I have talked non-stop and listened to my family and friends tell their tales of convincing me that they couldn't be here for Christmas. Which I have to admit, the old me would have been really pissed about, but I am a different person now, and all I feel is the love surrounding me, and how sweet and kind and thoughtful my man is for organising all of this.

And then I realise I have nothing to offer anyone. No party food, no nothing – *It was just supposed to be Tristan and me!* And now they're all here and have told me they'll all be here tomorrow too, there is no way I have enough food. I feel all the blood drain out of my face, and panic set in.

"Coral, whatever is the matter?" Gladys asks as she happens to be the one sitting next to me.

The champagne cocktail in my hand begins to shake, giving me away. "Food," Is all I manage to gasp, as I feel like I'm about to have an anxiety attack.

"Food?" Gladys questions.

"Tomorrow," I gasp again, 'I haven't got enough for everyone," I try taking several deep breaths, but it's not working – *I can't breathe!*

"Tristan," Gladys calls and begins ushering him over to her with manic hand gestures.

In seconds he's at my side. "Christ!" he runs his hands through his hair, "What's wrong baby?" he gently asks as he kneels down in front of me.

"She said something about food for tomorrow," Gladys says.

Tristan instantly relaxes. "Baby, it's all organised. Calm down," he gently says.

"Organised?" I balk, trying to get more air into my lungs. My heart feels like it's trying to crawl out of my throat.

"Let's go outside for a moment and get you some fresh air," Tristan says, he lifts me into his arms and carries me outside. "Some water Gladys?" he adds as he slides open the patio door.

Placing me down onto one of the chairs that have evidently been dried of rain, he takes my hands in his. "Deep breaths baby," he softly says.

Gladys appears with a glass of water and passes it to me.

## A Christmas Wish

"I know what she means," she says to Tristan, then kneels down in front of me – I manage to take a sip of water.

"Coral darling, we are all bringing food with us. You see, Tristan organised it, so we all have one food item to bring, which makes it so much easier for everyone, and it meant you weren't cooking all day love," Gladys reaches up and places her hand on my cheek, and smiles so softly at me. "The turkey is in our oven and will be ready for tomorrow. It's a big one too so there will be plenty to go around," she adds with a soft, loving smile.

I feel my heart start to calm, and my breathing slows down.

"Really?" I say, the ringing in my ears slowly subsiding.

"Yes darling," she laughs, 'you didn't think he'd organise all of this without thinking of that did you?"

I frown back at her. "Wait – what about tonight?" I whisper.

"All sorted," Tristan says, and gently runs his knuckle down my cheek. "Everyone has bought something with them," he adds.

"You don't have to worry about a thing," Gladys says and looks adoringly at Tristan, then back at me.

*Holy fuck!* - I take a deep calming breath. "It might have been a good idea to tell me that at the beginning of the surprise," I laugh, feeling lighter by the second.

Tristan chuckles along with me. "In hindsight, I should have," he agrees, then wraps his arm around my shoulder and pulls me into him so he can kiss my temple.

"I'll leave you to it," Gladys says, and with a kiss on my cheek, and one for Tristan, she walks back inside.

I turn to Tristan, feeling almost back to normal, and place my hand on his cheek. "Thank you, Tristan," I say with the utmost sincerity.

"You don't have to thank me," he replies and smiles his shy smile.

And all humour is gone. I place my other hand on his cheek and stare back at him. I can feel the intensity rolling off me like waves. "Tristan...you have made my Christmas wish come true, but even better than the one I had planned. I get to see my family and friends without the stress and the...' I'm lost for words, I take a deep breath as I try to think of words that would explain the depth of love I have for this man, and how much I love him for what he's done.

"I don't quite know how to thank you for that, because 'thank you' are just words, and what I feel right now, how happy

I feel, doesn't even come close to those words..." I shake my head as a few stray tears escape and laugh at my own idiocy.

"All for you," he whispers and smiles widely at me. "I knew how much you wanted this before you even knew you wanted this, but I wanted you to be able to enjoy it and relax, which you now can," he says.

And I wrap my arms around his neck and hold him tightly. As I do, I notice for the first time in many weeks that I can see the stars - we actually have a clear sky.

"Tristan, look," I say.

He pulls back and realising what I'm looking at, his gaze follows mine. "Northern Star," he whispers and smiles widely up at the sky.

I stand, and Tristan does the same, so we are side by side. I entwine my hand in his and squeeze it tight. "Merry Christmas baby," I whisper, looking up at the stars, and realising that even though the sky above is full of magic and wonder – it doesn't compare to Tristan.

"Merry Christmas," he whispers back and then turning away from the sky, his lips reach mine in a passionate kiss that takes my breath away...

THE PARTY IS in full swing. Everyone has eaten from the buffet of party food and are merrily getting tipsy, as one should on Christmas Eve. Christmas songs are blasting through the speakers, Rob, Gladys, Joyce and Debs are giving it large on the makeshift dance floor, which is basically the middle of the living room, as the sofa has been pushed back against the wall. Rob is pulling some hilarious dance moves, making me laugh out loud at his ludicrously. And then the track changes and I immediately recognise the song – Some Enchanted Evening.

"Boring!" Rob snorts loudly and walks over to Tristan's player to skip the track.

Tristan appears right next to Rob with his hands in his pockets, and without a word he slowly shakes his head from side to side, warning Rob who rolls his eyes in disgust, and stomps off to get another cocktail.

My very own James Bond stares at me from across the dance floor.

I smile widely at him.

He walks towards me in such a dashing way, he's reminding me of Cary Grant.

"May I have this dance?" he asks, bowing slightly.

# A Christmas Wish

"You may," I reply, playing along with his game and giving him a small curtsy of my own, as I place my hand in his. He escorts me to the middle of the room, and we begin to sway to our song.

And as we do, I get an image come into my mind's eye of a little boy, with chubby, rosy cheeks, bright green eyes, and curly brown hair, and he's smiling widely at me, and he's happy, and I suddenly realise who he is. Our child, our unborn child. And I know at that moment, I can feel it. I'm not afraid of being a mother anymore. The fear has been lifted with the most beautiful feeling of unconditional love. And then another image comes to mind – a memory of an old session with George.

*"We are all born into this world capable of one thing,"* George said.

*"And what's that?"* I asked.

*"Love,"* he replied.

And I'm back in the present again, still dancing in my husband's arms, and I can still see the baby's face, smiling at me. I look up at Tristan, who smiles down at me, and I know I will be a good mother because I have Tristan by my side. He would never let me do anything stupid, and for the first time in my life, I actually believe in myself, I believe that I can do this and that George is right - we do come into this world knowing only love, it's just everything else that fucks it up along the way.

"Once you have found her, never let her go," Tristan's voice brings me back to him as he sings the words to our song.

I smile up at him. "I bet you can't hit the high note at the end," I laugh.

He shakes his head and smiles that shy smile that I dearly love. "No way," he laughs, 'not even going to attempt it," he adds and swings me around, then as the song ends he tips me back, leans down and gently plants his lips on my neck...

# EPILOGUE

December 2015

AS I SIT WAITING impatiently for Dr Andrews, I can't help tapping my foot repeatedly, which begins to annoy a man that's sitting opposite me, reading his newspaper. Twice now he has looked up at me over his paper, as I sit chewing my nails with nerves unlike any other I have ever know.

I look down at my flat stomach again – *Christ! What have I done!*

"Mrs Freeman?" The receptionist calls out. I stand, with the speed of a bullet and with one quick nod to her, I dash down the hallway, then without knocking I barge into Dr Andrews' office, and slam the door shut behind me - *Christ I'm a gibbering wreck!*

"Coral!" he says, he's surprised to see me, and then his face falls as he sees the look on my face. "Come and take a' – "I think I'm pregnant!" I blurt. And burst into tears – *Crap!*

"Ok, well let's find out shall we?" He calmly says, and getting to his feet, he slowly ushers me to the chair opposite him, and I sit. "Now, first of all, Coral, I would like you to take a deep breath, and try to calm yourself down," he tells me.

I nod once and do exactly that, I take a deep one in and slowly blow it out – and then I freak out again because all that's doing is reminding me of those awful breathing classes that Debs went to. I went with her once, and I'd never been so bored in my life.

And I'm hyperventilating again.

"Coral," Dr Andrews voice is stern now, 'I would just like to say that if it turns out you are pregnant, this level of stress is no good for the baby."

That got my attention – I look down at my stomach again,

## A Christmas Wish

god knows how many times I have done that over the past week, then I look up at Dr A, and nod.

"Ok," I swallow hard. "I'm calm," I add. My mouth feels like all moisture has been sucked out of it. Dr A passes me a cup of water from his machine. "Thanks," I glug it all back.

"Ok then, now, I have a few questions' – "Dr Andrews, I know you're going to ask when was the last day of my period... but please don't. Can't we just do a test?" I ask.

"Well that's not how' – "This works?" I interrupt. "Ok, look. For the first time in my life, I have missed a period. I am on the combined pill, but I forgot to take the last five pills this month. Simply put, Tristan and I went away, and I didn't realise until the last day that I'd even forgotten them. Anyway, I get home not thinking anything more about it, which was two weeks ago. Then I realised five days ago, that I haven't had my period. So, each day I have taken a pregnancy test, and I'm getting a yes, every time. And then I looked online, and I've got other symptoms too," I say, and draw breath – *Fuck a duck!*

"And what are your other symptoms?" He asks calmly, too calmly – *Why isn't he freaking out like me?*

"Um...really heavy boobs, I'm tired no matter how much sleep I get, and I seem to have developed a taste for liquorice...I mean, I like liquorice, but I just don't seem to be able to stop' – "Coral," Dr A laughs, 'please try to slow down, or you're going to leave me no choice but to call Mr Freeman."

My mouth pops open – *Is he serious?*

He laughs again. "I can see you are clearly worried about' – "I'm not worried,' I interrupt, 'I just can't handle not knowing... you know. If my life is about to change, in such a massive way, then I want to know, I *need* to know," I take another breath, and see Dr A does not look happy. "Sorry," I quickly tag on the end – And I'm chewing my tips again.

"Here," he passes me a small, plastic see-through bottle, with a white plastic cap. 'I need a urine sample, down the hall and to your right."

I nod and stand. "Sorry," I whisper again, and head out of his office – *Calm Coral, calm!*

Once I'm done, I head back into his office and hand him the sample. "Alright then," he says as he places a long paper strip of some sort into my pee, waits a couple of seconds and begins nodding. "Well, Coral, from the looks of things – you are pregnant. But we'll take a blood sample now, and we should be able to get the results to you tomorrow." And I want to give Tristan a big kiss for getting us private care.

Dr A continues. "In the meantime, I will get you referred to Dr Abigail Wright, she will discuss all the does and don'ts and organise a midwife to guide you through. And she should be able to give you a transvaginal sonogram, see if we can see anything," he says, smiling broadly at me.

"A what?" I reply, which makes him smile wider.

He taps his keyboard, and a second later he turns his screen and shows me an image of what looks like a frigging dildo – my mouth drops open again.

"They're going to want to put that, in me?" I squeak in horror...

TRISTAN AND I ARE lying on our bed, both on our backs, head to head, as we gaze at the picture he's holding in his hand, which is an image of my very first scan, which I wouldn't go to without Tristan, so it didn't happen until January.

"Wow," he says, for the third time. "I don't think I can quite believe it," he whispers.

"Well, believe it, baby, because you're going to be a Papa," I softly say.

This makes him chuckle. "A Papa?"

"Yeah," I reply, liking the sound of that. "And I'm going to be a Moma," I add.

"Trust you to be different, no mommy and daddy in this house huh?" he replies dryly.

I turn and look up at him. "I actually really like Moma," I tell him.

"You do?" he says, surprised.

"Yeah babes, I really do," I say.

Tristan smiles widely at me, leans down and gently pecks my lips. "Moma and Papa it is then," he laughs.

"Tristan," I say, feeling worried about the conversation I had with my midwife. "I've been speaking to Georgina, and I... please don't get mad," I say before I continue.

"Get mad? – "Please..." I beg, and he nods his head. "I'm not going to the hospital to have the baby, Tristan. I want it here, in this house. It's been our home for two and a half years now, and I feel safe, happy, and most importantly, I feel relaxed here."

He's quiet and contemplative for a moment, and then he

nods, decision made. "Ok, but wouldn't you rather move into the new house before having the baby?" He asks.

I shake my head at him. "This house is filled with so many happy memories, that I want it to be here that our lives make the turning point, another change. We have the baby here and say goodbye to the life we had before, by beginning a new, exciting chapter in our new abode, with the new addition to our little family," I say.

Tristan smiles widely at me. "Are you really ready for this?" he says.

I burst out laughing. "I don't really have much choice, and neither do you!"

"True," he laughs.

"Besides, Edith, Gladys, Debs and Joyce can hardly wait. So I'm thinking we are going to have a lot of help from our family, and hopefully, we won't be so tired and worn out that we don't get time to appreciate it, or each other," I say with a wink, making Tristan chuckle at me...

TWENTY FOUR HOURS of frigging breathing like a lunatic with contractions that are making me feel as though I am splitting in two, and he's still not out. *Come on Ethan!* The pain is unlike anything I have ever known. Another contraction hits - *Fuuuuuuckkk!*

"Breathe Coral, breathe!" My midwife Georgie demands.

"Holy mother of God!" I shout, trying to breathe through it again. "Tristan I'm scared," I whimper. I'm sat in a squat position, with Tristan behind me, holding my hands. And I'm so thankful he's here, I have no idea how women go through this alone.

"I'm right here," he whispers, squeezing my hands tightly. "You can do this," he adds.

"Ok Coral – push!" Georgie tells me, and so I do, with all my might, hoping and praying this will be over soon, and that this is the last push – I am beyond tired.

"Keep pushing," she shouts.

"You can do it, baby," Tristan whispers in my ear, as I squeeze his hands so tightly, I'm surprised he's not screaming himself.

"Ok, lovely Coral – stop pushing now, babies crowning," she says, concentrating hard on the task. And I feel the strangest sensation down below, and then I hear it, his cry – *Ethan!*

"Is he out?" I cry out.

"Yes!" Georgie shouts in delight as she begins checking him over.

"Oh my god," Tristan chokes. Being taller, I'm guessing he can see Georgie working on our little man.

"Is he ok?" I cry, already worried.

"Everything is fine," Georgie says, smiling widely, and then she's leaning forward and passing me a little bundle that's wrapped up a white blanket.

Tristan starts crying his crazy man crying behind me, which makes me burst into tears. And the two of us, together, take hold of baby Ethan and cradle him in our arms.

"Hi Ethan," I whisper, as silent tears stream down my cheeks, I reach up and softly stroke his forehead, wondering if he's going to like it, as his Papa does. "I'm your Moma," I add, which makes Tristan do a funny laughing, crying, I'm so happy but so overwhelmed noise.

"And this big guy behind me, he's your Papa," Ethan stares up at Tristan then, as though he already understands what I'm saying.

"Hey little man," Tristan says, and goes to stroke Ethan, but his little hand grabs onto Tristan's finger making him catch his breath. "Wow," he says again. And for a man who can speak so eloquently, he must really be lost for words.

"Thank you," I whisper to Tristan as I continue to stroke Ethan's forehead. "You gave me something to live and fight for Tristan, a family. First you and me, and now..." I start crying again, and for once I'm not mad that I am crying because these are one hundred percent tears of joy.

"No Coral," Tristan chokes out, "Thank you, baby," he sniffs a couple of times. So I twist my head around to him, wanting so much to comfort him, and softly kiss his lips.

"You did it," he says, resting his forehead against mine.

"We did it," I whisper back.

Tristan gazes down at Ethan in wonder and awe.

"Here Tristan," I turn slightly and place Ethan in his Papa's strong arms.

"Hi," Tristan whispers, then gently plants a kiss on Ethan's forehead. And I smile, overwhelmed with joy at the sight of my husband, gently holding our baby in his arms, and I know this is it, the beginning of another new adventure together. And there's not a single part of me that's afraid - and it's all because of Tristan. So onwards we will go, and travel down this new path, that's going to be challenging, and tiring, but also full of joy and surprises and most of all, happiness...

## The End

Thank you so much for reading A Christmas Wish. I hope you enjoyed Coral and Tristan Christmas story as much as I enjoyed writing it. I wish you all a very Merry Christmas, and a Happy, Safe, and Prosperous New Year!

Did you enjoy this book?
If so, you can make a big difference.

Reviews are the most powerful tools in my arsenal when it comes to getting attention for my books. Much as I'd like to, I don't have the financial muscle of a New York Publisher. I can't take out full page ads in the newspaper, or put posters on the subway. But I do have something more powerful than that, and it's something that those publishers would kill to get their hands on.

**A committed and loyal bunch of readers.**

Honest reviews of my books help bring them to the attention of other readers like you. If you've enjoyed this book I would be very grateful if you could spend just five minutes leaving a review (it can be as short as you like) ) or simply rating the book on the Amazon.

I wholeheartedly thank you in advance.

## And once again from Coral, Tristan, and me have a very Merry Christmas!

### Join My Mailing List

Join my mailing list via my website www.clairdelaneyauthor.com for exclusive offers and competitions and to keep updated with future releases.

## Connect with me

Also, you can connect with me via social media. Or contact me via the email address below. I would love to answer your questions, or simply read your feedback and comments.

**FACEBOOK** - Clair Delaney Author
**TWITTER -** @CDelaney_Author
**INSTAGRAM** – ClairDelaneyAuthor
**PINTEREST** – Clair Delaney Author
**WEBSITE** - www.clairdelaneyauthor.com
**EMAIL** - clairdelaneyauthor@gmail.com

# ABOUT THE AUTHOR

CLAIR DELANEY is a former P.A who currently lives in rural Wales in the UK. From a very young age, Clair would always be found drawing pictures and writing an exciting story to go with those picture books. At five years of age she told her mother she wanted to work for Disney, that dream didn't pan out, but eventually, she found the courage to put pen to paper and write her first romance novel Fallen For Him. She is also the author of Freed By Him, Forever With Him and A Christmas Wish, Darkest Fears Christmas Special. When she is not writing Clair loves to read, listen to music, keep fit and take long walks with her dogs in the countryside.

A Christmas Wish - Copyright © 2018 Clair Delaney

The moral rights of the author have been asserted. All characters and events in this e-book other than those clearly in the public domain are fictitious and any resemblance to real persons, living or dead is purely coincidence - All right reserved. This e-book is copyright material and must not be copied, reproduced, transferred, distributed or used in any way except as specifically permitted in writing by the author, as allowed under the terms and conditions under which it was purchased or as strictly permitted by applicable law. Any unauthorised distribution or use of this text, maybe a direct infringement of the authors rights, and those responsible maybe liable in law accordingly

Printed in Great Britain
by Amazon